"How do you _____"
Mallory coo___

Jack gave her a sexy grin. "Strong and ca_____ the outside, yet soft and pliant within." He reached forward and grasped her glass, easing it out of her fingers. "Sort of like you," he murmured, tucking a strand of hair behind her ear.

His touch was warm and sexy, like the timbre of his voice. Mallory's nipples tightened beneath the scrap of silk she wore. If Jack kept this up, she'd lose what little semblance of control she possessed.

He placed his glass beside her own. "Unless of course, that is an act," he continued.

Ahh. He wanted to test her limits and see if she turned back into being uptight and frigid. He wanted to see who would run first. Poor Jack. He had no idea she was prepared to see this through to the end.

"Maybe it is an act. Maybe it isn't," she said lightly. "The point is, you're still not sure, are you?"

"Not yet." He leaned forward until his lips were mere inches from hers. "But the night's still young. And I *do* plan to find out...."

Blaze™

Dear Reader,

Would you dare to issue a sexual challenge to a man who intrigues you? Would you proposition a colleague at the risk of your job? Lawyer Mallory Sinclair is shocked to discover she would. And her oh-so-sexy associate, Jack Latham, isn't complaining. What starts as one erotic invitation, leads to another—and another! Until the fun and games end and Mallory and Jack must fight to hold on to forever.

Erotic Invitation is the first in the MIDNIGHT FANTASIES miniseries. But don't worry, there will be many more fantasies coming your way, written by some of Harlequin Blaze's most talented authors.

I hope *Erotic Invitation* inspires you to reach out and grab something or someone *you* desire. After all, Harlequin Blaze is about fulfilling dreams. And one of my dreams is to know people enjoy my work. So let me know what you think. Write to me at: P.O. Box 483, Purchase, NY 10577, or visit my Web site at www.carlyphillips.com. And check out www.tryblaze.com.

Until next time, enjoy!

Carly Phillips

Books by Carly Phillips

HARLEQUIN BLAZE
8—BODY HEAT

HARLEQUIN TEMPTATION
736—BRAZEN
775—SIMPLY SINFUL
779—SIMPLY SCANDALOUS
815—SIMPLY SENSUAL

EROTIC INVITATION

Carly Phillips

HARLEQUIN®

TORONTO • NEW YORK • LONDON
AMSTERDAM • PARIS • SYDNEY • HAMBURG
STOCKHOLM • ATHENS • TOKYO • MILAN • MADRID
PRAGUE • WARSAW • BUDAPEST • AUCKLAND

To my readers—special people who aren't afraid
to let their imaginations sweep them away.
Thanks for buying my books. This one's for you.

And to the Temptresses—who offer the best in daily support
and coffee-spewing moments of laughter.
What would I do without you? I'm proud to call you friends.

ISBN 0-373-79021-X

EROTIC INVITATION

Copyright © 2001 by Karen Drogin.

This edition published by arrangement with Harlequin Books S.A.

® and TM are trademarks of the publisher. Trademarks indicated with ® are registered in the United States Patent and Trademark Office, the Canadian Trade Marks Office and in other countries.

Visit us at www.eHarlequin.com

Printed in U.S.A.

1

"YOU'VE BEEN SUMMONED."

Mallory Sinclair glanced up from the complicated lease she'd been reading to find her secretary, Paula, standing in the doorway. "Sorry, I didn't hear you knock."

"That's because I didn't. When the Terminator calls there's no time to waste. Especially if you want a minute to freshen up before entering his lair." Paula, Mallory's young, beautiful and on-the-prowl secretary, wiggled her eyebrows in a suggestive gesture meant to prompt Mallory into primping for this unexpected meeting with the firm's best-looking partner.

Mallory reached for a legal pad instead of her purse. Though she'd never let her emotions show, for the first time in her eight years with Waldorf, Haynes, Greene, Meyers & Latham, she shook in her no-nonsense pumps. She'd fought for assignments, gone head-to-head with senior partners over issues she believed in, and she'd held on to her job when other female associates had quit, been fired or had moved on to get married or have a family. She was the sole surviving female in a male dominated arena and was only one year away from making partner. She hadn't gotten this far without confrontation and she'd never backed away from a fight. Never been afraid to work with or take on opposing counsel or partner. Until now.

Because as the top real estate associate, she'd never been summoned by hotshot divorce attorney and partner of the firm, Jack Latham. A man equal parts sexy male and lethal terminator—marriage terminator. That he wanted to see her now meant he had good reason.

"I could say you're busy and take notes in your place."

Mallory didn't miss the hopeful note in her flirtatious secretary's voice. The other woman envied Mallory's meeting with Jack Latham. He was an office icon—a man adored by women and respected by men.

If the grapevine was correct, he neither believed in the institution of marriage nor the idea of commitment. But his views weren't a deterrent to any breathing member of the opposite sex. Every woman in the office thought given the chance, she could change his mind.

"Thanks for the offer but I'm sure I can handle it." Mallory smiled wryly.

Paula shrugged. "Too bad. I could really use the distraction and give him a meeting he'd never forget." She hitched her already borderline-trouble skirt hem up another notch.

Mallory stifled a laugh. Good thing for Jack there was a no-office-romance policy, instituted after an employee had filed a sexual harassment suit against an older partner three years ago. The firm had settled quietly, the founding partner had retired, and the no-dating rule had gone into effect. Women like Paula could drool, but they couldn't put the moves on any of the male attorneys, and vice versa. But rules couldn't stop the imagination and there wasn't a woman in the office, from secretary, to paralegal, *to the only female associate,* who hadn't fantasized about Jack Latham.

The difference between Mallory and the other women in the office was that she didn't outwardly show interest. She couldn't afford to crack her facade. She glanced at Paula who sat twirling a permed blond strand of hair around one finger, a disappointed look on her face.

"If the man knew what I'd saved him from, he'd get down on his hands and knees and thank me," Mallory said.

"I wish he'd get down on those knees for me." Paula let out an exaggerated sigh before glancing at her watch. "You'd better get going. He said posthaste or something like that."

"Thanks." Pad under her arm, Mallory headed out of her office and down the hall.

She clenched her fists, only to discover she was sweating. Good God, she felt like a teenager in the throes of her first crush and that wouldn't do. Not when she'd done everything she could think of to join the ranks of this old boys' network and make partner.

Including outwardly suppressing her femininity. She hid her sexy lace teddies and garters beneath conservative suits, covered her hot-colored pedicures with sensible pumps, showed only unlacquered fingernails, and squashed her sense of humor and warmth beneath a no-nonsense personality. When she looked in the mirror she barely recognized the person staring back.

But next year, she'd reap the benefits of her sacrifice: she'd earn both the first female partnership offered at the firm, and her father's respect. The man who'd desired a son and gotten Mallory instead, would finally see she was worthy, despite his belief to the contrary.

She inhaled deeply. "I'm nearly there," she purposely said aloud, to remind herself of how hard she'd worked and how far she'd come. No way would she let a summons from Jack Latham, her secret fantasy, destroy a dream eight years in the making. She let out a long breath. Yes, she could handle Jack Latham.

She paused outside his office to wipe her palms against her skirt and smooth back her hair, then she knocked three times in rapid succession.

"Come on in." A deep sexy voice rumbled from behind the closed door.

Her stomach curled with a combination of warmth and anticipation. She reached for the doorknob and entered. But not before a last glimpse at her chest to make sure her sea-pearl buttons were closed tight and not a hint of lace or silk would make an unwanted appearance. She stepped into his office and shut the door.

Hands linked behind his back, Jack Latham stood at the window overlooking the scenery below, the Empire State Building, tall and imposing in the background.

His broad shoulders were covered by a navy pin-striped suit. European and designer-made, the jacket accented his powerful frame. He presented as potent a vision as the landscape outside the window. Fog surrounded the city; a New York summer day and the view from the corner office at its finest, Mallory thought.

He didn't turn when the door creaked behind her. She wasn't surprised. She knew the game, just as Jack knew who stood at his desk, awaiting his attention. He'd summoned her, after all. But to acknowledge her immediately might shift the balance of power toward equality and he wouldn't do that with an associate. Especially a female associate. Every time she was assigned a new partner, she underwent the same drill, and often asked herself if Intimidation 101 was a prerequisite for men working in the field of law.

She'd learned not to let it get to her and she'd learned to push back. She cleared her throat. "Excuse me, Mr. Latham, but you asked to see me?"

Silence.

Strange, she thought. But then what did she know of the man? Although he'd been at Waldorf, Haynes longer than she had, the firm boasted over seventy-five attorneys spread out over three floors of a high-rise building. Their paths had rarely crossed on a one-to-one basis. Until now.

One more try and she was out of here. He could come looking for her if he intended to carry this game too far. "Mr. Latham?"

THAT VOICE AGAIN. Softer than Jack had expected and at odds with the tough legal reputation Mallory

Sinclair attained, it penetrated the troubles muddling his thoughts. Her tone was smooth enough to appeal to a man's senses, and husky enough to remind him of fantasies involving hot nights beneath cool sheets.

He shook his head, clearing his mind. From all he'd seen and heard of Mallory Sinclair, she wasn't one to inspire seductive visions. And as he turned to Waldorf, Haynes's sole female associate, her appearance put him squarely back into office-mode. The woman standing before him was as hard as her voice was soft. From her severely pulled back hair, to her overly long skirt and conservative suit, she was every inch *not* his fantasy woman.

But she was the woman with whom he'd be confined at a resort owned by the firm's biggest client, off the coast of Long Island. For Lord knew how long.

Jack cleared his throat and met Mallory's gaze. Behind the black-rimmed glasses, she'd narrowed her eyes until he couldn't tell if they were a blue or a bland shade of gray. He'd obviously irritated her. He hadn't meant to get on her bad side from the get-go, and he hadn't meant to ignore her.

While waiting for her to arrive, his father had called and delivered a personal blow. Apparently, his beloved mother had embarked on another affair, this one more public than the last. And his tolerant, accepting dad, had finally walked out. Jack's stomach rolled to think his father was about to go through the kind of nasty divorce he specialized in, but it was about time. The marriage should never have lasted—

most didn't—and if not for his father's unending acceptance and patience, his mother would be on her own by now. Yet as bad as Jack felt for his father, he had no choice but to deal with family issues later.

Right now he had more immediate problems at hand. He stepped away from the window. "I was preoccupied," he explained to Mallory.

Her hands gripped the edge of his desk. "Obviously. I can always come back at a more convenient time. I have plenty of work sitting on my desk."

Work he'd obviously taken her away from and she wasn't pleased. He doubted she'd be any happier when she learned the reason for their last-minute meeting. "No, now's fine. Have a seat." He gestured to the wing chair in the corner, a congratulations gift from his father for making partner. His mother hadn't bothered to make it to his law school graduation, never mind acknowledging his career accomplishments.

Mallory lowered herself into the chair and crossed one leg over the other. His gaze fell to the shifting material of the skirt that covered way too much skin, even in this staid profession.

"So." Her voice captured his attention.

Amazing, Jack thought. When he wasn't focused on her plain features or tailored clothes, that husky voice wreaked havoc on his nerve endings, sending the wrong signals from his brain to parts of his body that had no business rising during office hours. He shifted uncomfortably in his seat.

"What can I do for you?" she asked.

"I'll be brief. I understand you're working on a

real estate deal, but I've arranged to shuffle your workload around to free you up. For me."

His words sent her into a frenzied fit of coughing. Concerned, Jack rose from his seat and came up beside her. "Are you okay?"

She removed her glasses and dabbed at her eyes with a tissue she'd grabbed from his desk. "Fine. I'm perfectly fine. I just swallowed wrong. Sorry about that." Obviously embarrassed, she cleared her throat and patted around her eyes once more before meeting his gaze.

In the instant those china-blue eyes met his, Jack felt as though he'd been sucker punched. His breath caught and he nearly went into a coughing fit of his own. Sweet heaven, someone should have warned him the woman had such expressive, gorgeous eyes. Before he could continue, she pushed the black frames back on and resettled the glasses on the bridge of her nose. Once again, thick lenses obscured his ability to see into her eyes, making him wonder if he'd imagined the depth and clarity of hue.

"What do you mean you've shuffled my workload? Didn't anyone tell you Mendelsohn Leasing requested I handle the negotiation on their newest land acquisition personally?"

He rounded his desk and resettled himself into his seat. At this point, he was off balance and uncertain of Mallory Sinclair, something he never felt with a woman or in business. Distance seemed the safest bet. "I assure you I was fully informed of the situation but we decided to weigh all involved interests and the scales tipped in Lederman's favor."

"Our biggest client. One who's been farming out business to other firms, leaving us vulnerable to losing an important money base."

So she was up on all firm business. "Yes. However this time we're not talking about a potential merger or acquisition but Lederman's divorce."

She inclined her head. "If you're involved, that much is obvious. What isn't clear is where I come in. You could pick any associate specializing in domestic or family law. You don't need me."

Jack leaned forward, elbows propped on his desk. "Now that's where you're wrong. Much as we both obviously wish differently, you're exactly what I need."

Mallory Sinclair hadn't been his first choice as an assistant, but he'd been outvoted. His partners felt a woman's presence would strengthen their position with the client and assure him of their willingness to play hardball against his wife. Jack couldn't argue the point. Waldorf, Haynes couldn't afford to lose Lederman's business and securing the role of counsel in this divorce was of paramount importance.

After a moment she let out a long breath of air. "Why don't you explain why you need me." She paused. "Please."

He picked up a pencil and twirled it between his palms. "It's simple. Lederman wants to win. He wants a team of attorneys who sympathize with him as a man whose wife wants to take him for a ride and who aren't afraid to play hardball to accomplish those goals. And we—the partners—feel his needs can best be met by having a female attorney sitting at his side.

And as you know, when there's direct contact with Mrs. Lederman, a woman dealing with another woman would give us greater strength. You could relate to her in a way I could not.''

He watched for the play of emotions sure to cross her face during his explanation. There were none. Whatever her thoughts, she kept them to herself. The woman knew how to play poker, Jack thought, and his respect for her rose. He could see now how she'd come so far with the older male guard at Waldorf, Haynes. But she hadn't earned their trust completely. He doubted any female ever could. This was an old boys' network and they weren't ashamed to admit it.

Jack didn't agree with their way of thinking on many issues, this one included. He didn't trust women in the marriage arena—his family background, client history and divorce statistics providing backup to his beliefs. But regardless of whether women were usually at fault on the domestic front, business was different. Skill alone determined whether Jack would trust their abilities. The old men weren't as easily swayed, but Mallory was useful to them. And she obviously knew it.

She nodded slowly. "So I'm yours by default. Being the only female associate, that is."

He couldn't help it. He grinned. "In a manner of speaking, yes." She was his. In all her tweed and glory.

From all he'd seen and heard, Mallory Sinclair was one of the best. But before they could get down to business, they were headed for an informal get-to-know-you-better session, demanded by their eccentric client. Based on Mallory's cool personality and severe looks, casual and relaxed wasn't her thing. Which meant Jack wasn't looking forward to their enforced time together.

Yet despite himself the memory of those china-blue eyes stayed with him. Intrigued him. Made him wonder what else he didn't know about Ms. Mallory Sinclair.

She rose from her seat. "Guess that means case closed, then."

"I'm sure we'll survive," he said, issuing a grin meant to ease things between them.

He waited for a smile in return and was disappointed not to get one. "I'll need to wrap some things up before I can start on Lederman's case," she said.

"No problem. Our flight leaves at 7:00 p.m. Think you can tie up loose ends, pack and be at the airport in…" he glanced at his watch. "Three hours?"

Her lipstick-free mouth opened, then closed again. He'd managed to get a reaction after all. "Our *flight?*" The word sounded more like a squeak.

He nodded. "Mr. Lederman is at his resort in the Hamptons. He doesn't care to cut his vacation short, so we're going to head on out there and get to know him. Grab your sunglasses and bathing suit. We're going to the beach."

MALLORY ROLLED her silk stockings down her legs slowly, savoring the sensation against her skin. She so missed the little luxuries in life—silk, satin and anything soft, which was why she always did her best to pamper herself beneath her conservative image.

Thanks to a spilled pocketbook-size vial of her favorite perfume, normally saved for evenings after work, the comforting aroma indulged her senses now. But neither the conservative attorney nor the buried woman were foolish enough to wear stockings to a hot, summer resort.

With Jack Latham.

She shivered at the unexpected prospect of spending hours in his company away from the office. She opened her suitcase and tossed it on the bed.

"Going somewhere exciting?" Her cousin Julia bounded into the room with all the exuberance of a college freshman. Or someone who would be a college freshman if she hadn't opted for a free-spirited route in life.

Just looking at her, Mallory felt old beyond her years. Mallory was still young enough to be carefree, it was just the external trappings that constrained her. And those couldn't be avoided. Not if she wanted to make partner.

"Hey, Mal. I asked you where you're off to?"

Mallory turned to her cousin. Their fathers were brothers, and by a strange mix of the gene pool, Julia and Mallory shared an uncanny resemblance, down to their blue eyes. Looking at her cousin was like looking in a mirror, minus a few years, chronological as well as emotional. Julia was a bundle of happiness, and like Mallory she was also a disappointment to her father. Unlike Mallory, she didn't feel the need to change her parent's opinion.

"I'm off to a sunny resort and before you get jealous, remember it's business." And with luck, Jack would remember that, too. He'd dress up and not down and even if their eccentric, bossy client insisted on a poolside meeting, Jack would *dress,* period. Because Mallory was afraid if she saw him bare-chested and tanned, in swimming trunks that accentuated and revealed, she couldn't be responsible for her actions.

And Mallory Sinclair was always the upstanding, responsible adult and attorney. Always. She had to be.

Julia sat on the bed and crossed her legs. "It may be business, but it's still the beach."

"That's what Jack said." The memory of his charcoal-gray eyes boring into hers lit a fire inside her. The warmth of desire burst into a burning flame. Lust, Mallory reminded herself. Nothing more than sexual need, a desire easily controlled. No matter if she was lying to herself, she had no choice but to convince herself and act accordingly. So what if the man was sexy? She was an adult, after all.

"Who's Jack?"

"The senior partner in charge of this case." Her garment bag already packed with a combination of appropriate lightweight pantsuits and skirts, Mallory folded her private underthings and placed them inside the suitcase.

Julia seated herself on the bed. "What's he look like?"

"What's it matter?" Mallory shot back quickly.

Too quickly, and her cousin's eyes narrowed. "Why so testy? Uptight about going away with a sev-

enty-year-old man who's judging your every move?''
Julia's blue eyes locked with hers, daring her to reveal
what was on her mind.

Sometimes Julia was too perceptive and understanding, just another reason why Mallory adored her
cousin and let her live here rent-free while she ''found
herself'' in New York. ''More like a thirty-something,
perfect-looking, unattached man,'' Mallory muttered.

Julia laughed. ''I heard that.''

''I wanted you to or I wouldn't have spoken out
loud.''

''That's my favorite cousin, nothing uncalculated,
nothing unplanned.''

''The complete opposite of your spontaneous nature, you mean. You know it wouldn't hurt you to
plan ahead. Set goals, chart your course in life.''

''Any more than it would hurt you to jump into
something with your heart and not your head. So
what's the story with your office hunk?''

Mallory shook her head. ''No story. Not with a no-
office-romance policy, and not with a man who, if
you believe the rumors, doesn't have the ability to
commit.'' And not with a man who hadn't shown her
an ounce of interest.

Julia leaned forward, resting on her elbows and
propping her chin on her palms. ''So? Does he have
to commit to have an affair?''

''Who said I was looking for an affair?'' Or a commitment for that matter. She didn't have the time to
worry about her personal life, at least not until her
partnership was secure and stable.

"Maybe you should be." Julia reached into the suitcase and held one of Mallory's lace teddy's in the air, dangling it from her fingertips. "Seems to me these lacy getups are wasted if you're alone."

Mallory grabbed for her nightie and buried it back inside her suitcase where it belonged. "Didn't you ever hear of doing things for yourself?"

"Anyone ever tell you it's more fun doing it with a partner?"

Visions of herself and Jack played before her eyes, a seductive dance with the ocean as the backdrop. She shook her head at her thoughts—all inappropriate, uncalled for and not possible. Beyond office policy and Mallory's long-term goals, she understood reality.

She swung the suitcase off the bed and blew Julia a kiss. "I'll be in touch." She passed the mirror as she headed out the door, catching a glimpse of herself in the glass. Her black glasses stood out, glaring and unattractive. Exactly as she'd meant them to be.

Mallory was heading off to an exclusive resort with the best-looking man she'd ever met. A man who made her ache with a simple glance. A man whose voice caused ripples of awareness to burst to life inside her.

But just as she planned, that sexy man wouldn't give her an interested glance. Jack Latham wouldn't be captivated by Mallory Sinclair, attorney. He wouldn't be charmed, enchanted or tempted.

"It might help if you let down your hair," her cousin supplied in a sugary-helpful voice.

Not if she wanted to make partner. Mallory glanced

at her watch. Half an hour till show time. She had a
firm-hired car picking her up downstairs to take her
to the airport. "Gotta run or I'll be late."

"Don't do anything I wouldn't do."

"It's not like I'll even be given the chance," she
muttered to herself.

2

JACK GLANCED at his watch. Half an hour until landing and their descent couldn't come a minute too soon. He didn't know how much more togetherness he could take. Mallory shifted in her seat and her right knee grazed his left leg. A shot of heat radiated up his thigh.

"Sorry," she mumbled, then sighed.

It had been like this for the entire flight. The cramped quarters of the plane and Mallory's enforced proximity was causing his body to react in conflicting and confounding ways. She'd exchanged the uptight suit for a lightweight dress with a hem that ended marginally higher and revealed an enticing hint of bare skin. Without stockings he was treated to tanned, smooth-looking flesh and he found his gaze drawn back again and again.

He assumed her contradiction in dress, along with the arousing floral scent that had permeated the cabin from the moment of her punctual arrival accounted for his curiosity. He wasn't about to call what he felt for Mallory *interest.*

But he hadn't noticed her feminine fragrance in his office earlier that afternoon, and he couldn't help but wonder about a woman who dressed and acted with an ultraconservative flair, yet managed to unwittingly tease a man with her voice and affect him with her scent. A woman who could entice with an innocent, accidental brush of bare skin.

"So what's the plan when we arrive?" Mallory asked.

Grateful for normal conversation at last, he turned toward her. "Lederman has a car meeting us at the airport. We should be at the resort by nine. I assume we'll unpack and get some sleep. After that, it's up to our host what happens next."

"With any luck we can discuss his plans, lay out strategy and be home in a couple of days."

He didn't miss the hopeful note in her husky voice. "What do you have against the beach?"

"Nothing if you're on vacation. But every day we're out of the office means work is piling up." Her jaw ticked in frustration.

He leaned back in his seat. "That's why I had the bulk of your work reassigned. Paul Lederman is eccentric. He doesn't like to be rushed and if he's refusing to leave the resort to meet with us in the office, I wouldn't hold my breath for a quick decision on his part."

She muttered something he didn't catch and he shifted his gaze from the drawn window shades to her face, taking in her profile for the first time. Severe hair and black glasses aside, she had chiseled features, high cheekbones and even minus the makeup, porcelain skin most actresses and models would kill to possess. But she did nothing to enhance her looks. In fact, she did everything possible to detract from them. He wondered why.

He shrugged and transferred his gaze. This flight was definitely too damn long if he was looking beyond the surface and contemplating Mallory Sinclair's grooming habits.

"What are the basic facts of the case?" As she spoke, she leaned down and pulled a yellow legal pad from her briefcase, then grabbed for a pen. "Ready when you are." She sat up straight in her seat.

The woman was brusque and efficient, the way he liked his associates. But not his women. Women, he preferred soft and pliant, warm and giving. With at least a week at a resort ahead of him, there'd be no shortage of the opposite sex. Unfortunately, strangers no longer appealed to him, which meant life was becoming increasingly complicated.

A short, no-strings affair suited his lifestyle and beliefs best. He couldn't end up in divorce court as anything other than counsel if he lived by his self-imposed rules. With no commitments, he couldn't be the cuckolded, sad excuse for a man his father had become. But with age came wisdom and discrimination—and an increasing restlessness he couldn't understand.

"Mr. Latham? Is something wrong?"

At the sound of her lush tone, a ripple of awareness meandered through his veins. A trickling, growing warmth pulsed in his groin. Something was wrong, all right. Everything he was feeling about his associate was off-kilter and he didn't like it one bit.

"What did you want?" he bit out.

"The facts of the case." She waved the legal pad in the air, reminding him of why they were together on the plane. "I want to be up on things to help impress the client."

He met her gaze behind the thick lenses. Sanity returned and he immediately felt better. "You might as well call me Jack."

She nodded, wide-eyed.

He forced his stare away from the blue eyes he couldn't see clearly. "Lederman's been married for years. He's fifty-eight and wants out."

"Why?" She paused, pen ready to write down his every word.

"Irreconcilable differences."

"That's the legal definition. What's the behind-the-scenes take on things? What will boost the settlement in his favor? Assuming we get the case."

Jack stretched his legs out in front of him as much as he could, but made sure he didn't touch Mallory as he moved. "That's what we're here to find out. Then we decide how to take her faults and spin them in our client's favor."

"Interesting turn of phrase—*her* fault."

"How so?"

She crossed her legs in front of her, and his gaze fell to her ankles. He'd never been a leg man, but she made him rethink his preference.

"You're assuming it was Mrs. Lederman's fault that the marriage disintegrated. There's always the possibility that our client was equally to blame. And if that's the case, we need to put a positive spin on *his* negative actions."

He leaned his head against the seat and turned toward her. "That's what I said. We need to put a positive spin on things."

"You said we need to spin *her* faults..." Her voice trailed off, and she shook her head before capping her pen. "Never mind."

"I'm not sure I get the distinction you're trying to make."

She let out a long-suffering sigh. "I'm sure you don't." She busied herself putting away her things and latching her briefcase.

"Good afternoon, folks." A voice sounded on the loudspeaker, from the cockpit of the small plane. "We're about ready to begin our descent, so go ahead and fasten your seatbelts..."

The captain's voice prevented any further talk. Mallory checked her safety belt and stared out the window. She obviously had no desire to finish their conversation. Yet she'd gone and given him an odd, empty feeling in his gut. As though in the brief minutes of their discussion, she'd judged him and found him lacking.

He didn't like the sensation of coming up short in her estimation and he wasn't sure why. Once again, she had him off balance, only this time she'd left him with the burning desire to shift both her negative opinion as well as her lack of interest.

Jack loved a challenge, but he only acted when that challenge made sense. And his interest in Mallory Sinclair did not.

A WARM BREEZE blew off the ocean, carrying the scent of salt water in the air. Mallory's hair frizzed in the humidity, destroying the bun she'd worked hard to make earlier this morning. She glanced at her watch. It was 8:00 a.m. and there was still no sign of their host.

"He'll be here," Jack said in response to her unspoken aggravation. "He said to go ahead and have breakfast and he'd meet up with us by the time we were finished."

She raised her gaze from the cinnamon-raisin French toast on her plate to glance at Jack's face—something she'd been avoiding doing all morning. If she'd thought him devastating in a suit, he was overwhelmingly handsome in khaki shorts and a collared, short-sleeved shirt. Powerful muscles flexed in his arms and tanned skin peeked through the open buttons over his chest. His jet-black hair had been combed neatly back, and a pair of Oakley sunglasses covered his piercing gray eyes. He was perfection in a masculine package while she was a frizzy mess of conservatism in a bland, navy dress.

Oh, well. She wasn't here to impress Jack with her looks, she was here to dazzle both him and the client with her brains. If only she could pull her thoughts off his sexy frame and focus on the task ahead of them. She'd spent last night in her room across from his, tossing and turning, unable to sleep. Unable to forget the scent of his musky cologne or his deep, rumbling voice.

"Glad you could make it. So what do you think of my place?" A booming male voice interrupted her inappropriate thoughts before she could take them to the sensual conclusion she'd experienced in her dreams.

"It's incredible, but then you already know that." Jack rose from his seat and Mallory followed suit. "Makes me realize I'm in the wrong line of work," Jack said and laughed.

"You're welcome out here any time," a burly man said. "Now help me get rid of the albatross I married and I'll name a suite after you and this colleague of yours."

Mallory did her best not to wince at the callous words he used to describe his wife. The woman he'd married, for better or worse. The woman she assumed he'd once loved.

"Paul Lederman meet Mallory Sinclair, one of our top associates. Mallory, Paul Lederman." Jack gestured between Mallory and their client who was dressed even more informally than Jack in boxerlike bathing trunks. Eccentric was putting it mildly, she thought.

She extended her hand. "Nice to meet you at last, Mr. Lederman."

"Call me Paul." He pumped her hand with enthusiasm. "Can't be so formal while sitting at the beach and looking at this view."

She glanced over his shoulder, taking in the clear blue sky and the glistening water in the background. He was right. She'd been so caught up in *not* watching Jack, she'd all but ignored the beauty in front of her. "You're a lucky man, Mr. Lederman."

He corrected her with a shake of his head.

"I mean Paul. Jack's right. This place is incredible."

"Then after we talk, make sure you let loose and enjoy it a bit. I like my attorneys on the same wavelength as I am." He pulled out a chair and joined them at the table beneath the large umbrella. "Marriage." He shook his head. "Risky business."

Mallory grabbed for her pad and pen, while Jack leaned back in his seat. "Yours made it twenty-five years. Something must have held you two together," Jack said.

Mallory liked the fact that Jack didn't automatically bow to Lederman's point of view, even if he silently agreed with the man.

"My money," Lederman muttered.

"And children," Jack added.

"The kids are on their own now."

"So what are you looking for?" Mallory asked. "A quick out or..."

She didn't get a chance to finish before he picked up speed. "I don't care about quick. I just don't want to be taken for all I've got. All I've worked for my whole life."

"Does your wife work?" she asked.

"Hell no. Unless you count spending my money work."

"What about raising your kids, Paul? When did that stop counting for something?" a female voice asked.

Mallory looked up.

An older but still beautiful brunette stood behind Paul Lederman. "And what about catering your parties? Seeing to your important guests? Your whims? Your needs? Your health?'' The woman met Mallory's gaze in an obvious search for feminine understanding.

In the brown depths, Mallory glimpsed a sadness and weariness that tore at her heart. Without knowing all the facts, Mallory imagined Mrs. Lederman as a woman much like her own mother, who sacrificed everything in order to further her husband's desires. If her mother had focused even for a moment on anything other than her husband, she might have taken notice of the daughter she'd borne, then ignored when her father had decreed her a disappointment. With a sigh, Mallory shook off the personal memories, but her heart went out to Mrs. Lederman.

But she couldn't afford to pity her client's wife. Not if she was going to convince the man she could represent him to the best of her abilities. With difficulty, Mallory tore her gaze away from the woman's pleading expression and focused on her client instead.

She couldn't read the man or his feelings for his soon-to-be ex-wife. But she did see an aging man with a slight paunch and receding hairline who was married to an elegant, attractive woman who still desired to be his wife.

''I suggest you two do all communication through your attorneys from now on,'' Jack said, in a kind but firm voice.

Mallory glanced up through hooded eyes. The sadness in Mrs. Lederman's countenance grew.

''I didn't realize you'd already hired yours,'' his wife said.

Paul Lederman coughed once. "I haven't finalized a decision yet."

"But that doesn't mean you shouldn't protect yourself," Mallory advised.

He nodded. "The lady's got a point because I'm hiring the best."

Mallory recognized Lederman's subtle implication that he hadn't yet decided if Waldorf, Haynes deserved the job, but right now her focus was on Mrs. Lederman and her pain.

"You don't scare me, Paul. I'm looking at a man who doesn't recognize the best when he's got it in his life." To the other woman's credit, she held her emotions in check as best she could before she walked away, head held high.

"I didn't realize you were still living together," Jack said, breaking the awkward silence that followed.

Lederman snorted. "Not together. Opposite sides of the resort. She won't leave. Says she loves me but what she really means is she won't be charged with desertion. From her point of view, what's mine is hers and what's hers is hers. Damn place is turning into the War of the Roses."

He shot to his feet quickly, pushing his chair back hard. "And I want someone who can get me the hell out of it without a dent in my wallet." Muttering to himself, the older man stalked off, leaving Jack and Mallory alone.

"Dammit." Jack groaned and ran a hand through his hair. "He's explosive. I don't want to lose this client."

Mallory nodded. "Even if we get the case, with his personality if we can't control him, she'll come off looking sympathetic." Which the other woman most definitely was, Mallory thought.

But she schooled her face into the blank mask she'd perfected over the years, careful not to reveal her inner turmoil to Jack. He was a partner and had a vote in whether or not she became one as well. There was no way she could afford to show weakness now, especially gender-oriented weakness.

She tapped her pencil against her pad. "There's a story behind every sympathetic façade. Maybe Mrs. Lederman has a lover."

Jack raised an eyebrow. Although Mallory had been called in on this case because of her gender, he'd expected to battle some form of feminine empathy while working along with her. Instead she was wholly focused on their client's needs. He ought to be impressed, but her coolness bothered him in ways he didn't understand. After all, didn't he already know she was ambitious?

"What if it's Mr. Lederman who's cheating?" he asked, curious as to how she'd get around the hypothetical dilemma.

Mallory shrugged. "It all comes down to power. Whoever's got the most power—in this case, money and strength of will—wins. It doesn't look like we'll get much of a fight out of Mrs. Lederman." She paused in thought.

For a brief moment, even behind her glasses, her eyes clouded over and Jack clung to the hope she'd crack. Show some sign of feminine emotion. But just as quickly, the glimmer disappeared and Mallory met his gaze head-on, determination on her face. "We ought to take advantage of the fact that she doesn't seem to want the divorce," she said. "Use that to our advantage in convincing Lederman we've got the best strategy."

"She doesn't want the divorce yet. If she gets hit hard she'll probably hire an attorney who will come out swinging."

"Exactly." Mallory's voice rose in pitch, excitement infusing her tone as well as her spirit.

He could see now why she was so good at her job. Because she truly loved the nitty-gritty details and the opportunity to work out solutions to a client's benefit. He understood because he felt the same rush of adrenaline each time a case or an idea came to a successful conclusion. "So what do you propose?"

"We need to strike first and the only way we can do that is by winning control of this case. I'll call Rogers and see what kind of dirt he can dig up on Mrs. Lederman and her past. In the meantime, you question Mr. Lederman. I mean Paul. He's more likely to open up to you anyway. Male bonding and all that."

A grin edged the corners of his mouth. He couldn't help it. She was a bossy thing when she got revved up and he enjoyed her take-charge attitude. "Any other orders?"

An unexpected flush stained her cheeks. From pale to cherry in a matter of seconds. So warm blood ran through those veins after all. For a brief moment, he wondered just how hot he could get that blood pumping. Until he refocused and realized this was Mallory he was daydreaming about. His staid, uptight, probably repressed colleague.

He definitely needed to hook up with a woman and soon. Sexual drought. There was no other explanation for the bizarre reactions he was having toward his associate.

She shook her head. "Sorry. I'm not sure what I was thinking."

"Actually I'd say you were on target and thinking clearly. You go ahead and call the private investigator. If Lederman sees we're investing time and money in him without a guarantee, he's likely to be impressed. And I'm positive I can sway him before this trip is out."

"Really? I mean, great! I'll get on it." Her surprise was tangible.

Given her probable history with the other partners in the firm, he understood. But he wasn't one to knock a good idea just because it hadn't come from him. Her ideas were solid and her train of thought followed his. They'd make a good team.

A good *working* team, he amended. "You do that."

She met his gaze and nodded. She held his stare a minute too long.

He was unable to break the connection, but she had no problem. As she'd done many times this morning, her intense gaze darted from his, guiltily, as if she were a kid who'd gotten caught doing something naughty.

What a bundle of contradictions she was. He

doubted he'd ever understand her. It was probably best he never did. Because she drove him to distraction, causing him to question himself and his feelings. Why did he care what Mallory thought or felt as long as she did her job and did it well? Why did he have this strong, lingering desire to see if she possessed a feminine side? Why the hell did he need to know she had the emotions and the ability to empathize with a woman Jack would ultimately screw in a divorce settlement?

His feelings regarding Mallory Sinclair made no sense. Though Jack doubted Lederman was blameless, he was certain Mallory was right. If they dug deep enough, they'd uncover dirt on Mrs. Lederman and probably force her hand—which by implication would win Lederman over.

But Mallory's callous disregard of the other woman's plight stayed with him. And Jack knew why. Her single-minded determination to succeed at all costs reminded him of his mother's tenacity at taking what she wanted outside her marriage, regardless of the repercussions to his father. A strange analogy, maybe but one that was alive and glaring.

One that gave him the urge to see how far she would go in the name of her job. He leaned forward. "Mallory."

She paused from collecting her things. "Yes?"

"If you run into Mrs. Lederman and chances are good you will…"

She rose from her seat. "Don't worry, Jack. I can handle her." She paused, then drew a deep breath.

"Reach out to the tentative vulnerable wife we just saw. Woman-to-woman, you know?"

Jack closed his eyes. He knew. It was the exact reason she'd been chosen for this case. But hearing her say it so callously, as if she had no empathy at all for Mrs. Lederman, gave him an impression of Mallory he didn't want to believe. The professional part of him was impressed but the man in him yearned to see she was human, that she felt at least a feminine kinship for Mrs. Lederman even if she couldn't act on those feelings.

And he still wanted to know she wasn't as cold and calculating as she appeared. "You make it sound like you'd hit her up with false sympathy anywhere, including the ladies room."

She paused, as if contemplating his words and her delay in answering gave him hope.

"If that's what it took to win this client over, then yes. I would," she said at last.

So much for hope, he thought, disappointed beyond words. "Geez, lady, you're cold. Just once on this trip I'd like to see the woman beneath the frigid façade."

She stiffened and Jack cursed. He hadn't meant to speak aloud, nor had he meant to insult her. He just couldn't understand the conflicting emotions she inspired in him. But it wasn't an excuse and he doubted she'd understand.

She held the pad against her chest. "I take it that wasn't a compliment."

That much was obvious. "Look, I meant nothing by it. It was just a thoughtless..."

"Tactless, male remark. No offense taken." But her lips trembled as she spoke.

He didn't believe her. Though she hadn't run off in tears and her strength impressed him, he'd finally managed to crack the frigid mask she'd pasted on her face. This time she wasn't able to hide the pain his words caused her.

He felt lower than a snake. He'd gotten his wish. He hadn't seen her feminine side but he knew one existed. Unfortunately getting his wish held little satisfaction right now and not only because he'd hurt her. But because in causing her pain, he'd learned something about himself and Mallory. He cared about her feelings—something that was rare for him when dealing with women.

He hated phony tears. He hated when a woman played on his sympathy because he'd supposedly hurt her tender feelings. His mother was an expert at playing his father. And Jack had always sworn he'd never be the vulnerable one. To accomplish that goal, he couldn't let himself care.

He glanced at Mallory's face. She'd managed to plaster on a fake smile. One he didn't buy for a second. And that bothered him. A lot.

"See you." She turned and walked away, blue skirt hanging too low around her legs, hair pulled back in an unattractive bun.

"Shit," Jack said loud and clear. He glanced around the beach, which had filled up with women. Scantily clad women. Single women.

If Mallory appealed to him on so many levels there had to be a reason.

Maybe he just needed to get laid.

3

SO HE WANTED to see the woman behind the *frigid façade* did he? Mallory jerked open and slammed closed the drawers in her room, tossing things on the bed and muttering aloud.

Cold. He'd had the nerve to call her cold. She picked up her most sinful, decadent teddy and held it in the air. Could she really be cold, *frigid,* she amended if her taste ran to silk and satin? To warm brandy and smooth sheets? To erotic dreams she couldn't share with anyone, including the man who inspired them?

She pushed the pile of lingerie aside and flopped down on the bed. Her fist curled around the bedspread and she swiped at a stray tear that dripped down her face. God, the man had a way of getting to her. Sexually, emotionally, it didn't matter. She cared what he thought of her and hated, *hated* that all he saw was Mallory Sinclair, Esq. A woman she'd created to achieve her long-standing goal.

A goal that suddenly came in second to showing Jack Latham his hunch was right. The man obviously sensed there was more to Mallory than what the world saw. What *he* saw. Just as she believed there was more to Jack Latham than his Terminator moniker implied.

But the old double standard had come into play and Jack had actually criticized her for doing her job as well as any man. Mallory might not like her father's outlook on many things, but her parents had still ingrained her with some values she both admired and lived by. Including loyalty, respect and staying power—in relationships as well as careers. So here she was attempting to do her best for a man who was obviously hurting his wife. His treatment of Mrs. Lederman didn't, or shouldn't, matter, not to the professionals hired to represent him in a divorce. And that's what Mallory was. A professional.

Jack ought to understand because they were bound by the same ethics. Yet because she was a woman he expected her to act differently. To show her emotions. Coming from Jack, that damn double standard hurt. She'd expected more of him though she didn't know why. The man was the Terminator, after all. He represented husbands against wives regardless of fairness or truth. Because that was his ethical obligation.

But despite his job as Waldorf, Haynes's chief divorce attorney, Mallory believed there was more to Jack. Just one day in his company and she sensed a gold mine of emotion beneath the surface. Oh, if pushed, he would claim to believe in all his male clients. He would state aloud that women were at fault in the breakup of most marriages. She'd heard him spout the same rhetoric around the office. She couldn't help hearing his secretary's gossip about why he'd become a hotshot divorce attorney. If the stories regarding his mother's blatant and ongoing infidelities were true, then personal pain lay behind Jack's antimarriage rhetoric.

His shaded sunglasses had hidden his eyes but other things had given his emotions away. The twitch in his full lips and the grip of his hand on the table that turned his knuckles white, only obvious because she'd been looking for a sign of humanity, had proven Mallory correct. He wasn't immune to Mrs. Lederman's suffering, even as he directed her to communicate with the husband she loved through their attorneys from now on.

It had been easier to ignore Jack Latham's appeal when only sexual attraction was involved. Now that Mallory had spent time with the man, now that she saw depth behind the good looks and toned body, she couldn't leave him with the impression he obviously had of her. He wanted to see the woman behind the mask. And she had enough pride to want to strip away the veneer and show him.

It was a gamble. Jack Latham was a respected partner. He could break her career with a word whispered in the right ears. But weighing all risks, Mallory came down on the side of chance.

Geez, lady, you're cold. Just once on this trip I'd like to see the woman beneath the frigid façade.

She fingered a garment of pure silk between her fingertips. If he was perceptive enough to use that sort of terminology, Mallory was gutsy enough to expose what lay beneath.

For his eyes only.

Curling her legs beneath her, Mallory gave serious

thought to how best make her point. By the time she'd formulated her plan, she'd actually managed to arouse herself with tantalizing, intriguing possibilities.

She glanced at her watch. She had some free time before meeting up with Jack again later. Plenty of opportunity to set things in motion.

She lay back against the pillows, squeezed her eyes shut tight and imagined Jack's reaction. Anticipation rose inside her, building to a rolling crescendo, causing a steady, rhythmic pounding beat between her thighs. She lay her hand on the soft material of her panties. A small press downward both alleviated the ache and increased her need. Her fingertips glided over silk, outlining her mound of flesh. So easily, she thought. She could take the edge off the hunger and go on with her day. But alleviating her tension would kill the anticipation she'd feel watching Jack.

She wanted to make him need Mallory Sinclair, the woman.

Then she wanted to take him to the edge...and over.

And she wanted to topple with him, not alone.

So, Mallory thought, let the seduction begin.

HE COULD get used to this. Jack glanced out over the pool to the glistening water beyond. The tangy smell of the ocean, the clear blue sky and the sexy women in bikinis. Yeah, he could get used to this. He leaned back in his seat and stretched his legs out in front of him. The sun beat against his skin, warm and comforting.

"Sorry I'm late. I had to run a few errands and

they took longer than I thought.'' Mallory slid into the seat across from him, looking uptight in the same boxy blue dress. But she didn't seem upset over this morning's incident and he was grateful.

''Everything okay?''

She nodded. ''We left in such a rush that I forgot a few things.''

''Well I managed to catch up with Paul in the sauna. We spent an hour commiserating over needy women. It's way too soon to push him on making a decision, but he's starting to trust me and I've got some more facts to fill you in on.''

''Sounds good.''

''Drink first?'' he asked.

She hesitated.

''Consider this more a vacation than a business trip. Seriously we're only here because Lederman wants to get to know us outside of the office. He's eccentric, like I said. So go ahead. Have a drink.'' Jack wanted to put her at ease. There was no way he could spend a week in her company if she looked like she was about to bolt at the first opportunity.

After his thoughtless comment this morning, he wouldn't touch the issue of her clothes now, but he didn't know how long he could watch her roasting in dresses beneath the blazing sun.

He gestured for a waiter. ''The lady will have a...'' He narrowed his gaze, trying to assess what Ms. Sinclair would drink. ''White wine spritzer?''

She shook her head. ''Club soda, please.''

Jack blinked, and refrained from rolling his eyes.

"I'll have a refill." He lifted his glass that had contained Absolut vodka on the rocks.

The waiter nodded. "Be right back, folks."

"Oh, wait," Mallory said.

He turned back around. "Change your mind?"

Jack actually held his breath.

"A wedge of lime, please."

He should have known.

"So what were you saying about Lederman?" she asked.

"Aside from complaining about marriage, he's hiding something." Jack finished the end of his drink.

"What makes you say that?"

"He got a phone call. The guy who relayed the message didn't say who was calling, but Lederman bolted out of the sauna so fast he nearly lost his towel." He laughed and waited for her to do the same.

Her expression remained steady. He stifled a groan. He couldn't imagine she didn't find the image amusing, so he figured she was still angry with him after all. But he wasn't about to repeat this morning's conversation.

Better to focus on work. "At any rate, when he returned I asked him if everything was okay. I thought maybe there was an emergency at the resort, but he didn't cover well. He flushed, hemmed and hawed, then finally said his son had called from California."

Mallory shrugged. "Why are you so sure he didn't?"

"Gut instinct. Besides that's an easy enough answer without beating around the bush."

She nodded. "True. So what do you think he's hiding? It makes no sense to keep us in the dark. Not if we're on his side."

"Agreed. And I intend to find out just as soon as…"

"Here are your drinks, folks."

The waiter exchanged Jack's empty glass for a full one that no longer appealed, but he thanked the man and turned his gaze back to Mallory. "I could have outright asked him what was going on, but…"

"Excuse me sir, but this is for you." The waiter handed Jack a folded slip of paper.

"Phone message?" Jack wondered aloud.

"Actually the bartender asked me if I recognized the name on the top and since you'd just signed for your lunch earlier…"

"Did he say who left it?"

"He found it on the bar when the lunch crowd disappeared."

"Strange." He lifted the folded paper and a feminine scent drifted toward him. He raised the paper and the aroma grew stronger. More appealing.

"Anything else?" the waiter asked.

"No thank you," Mallory said in her polite but husky voice.

Jack shook his head, then unsealed the note. *Invitation to Seduction—a private evening of dinner, dancing and gratification of the senses. Eight o'clock. Beach cabin number 10.* He tried to swallow and choked instead. There were further instructions, seductive allusions about what he could expect should he dare to RSVP.

He flipped the page over and read the back print. *Come on time. And come hungry.* His eyes teared and he grabbed for the drink that hadn't appealed to him minutes earlier. Instead of easing his distress, the alcohol burned its way down his throat, and he coughed harder.

Mallory stood and gestured for the waiter. "Water, please," Jack heard her request. "Are you okay?" she asked.

He swallowed again and breathing came easier. "Fine. Just…swallowed wrong."

"Oh." She lowered herself into her seat. "You scared me for a second. I thought I was going to have to do mouth-to-mouth."

He stared at her, sure he hadn't heard correctly.

"Resuscitation," she said quickly. "Mouth-to-mouth resuscitation because I thought you'd stopped breathing or something." She waved her hand in the air. "Never mind. As long as you're okay now."

"I'm fine." He glanced at the note that now lay in his lap. As fine as he could be with an erotic invitation to seduction nestled in his groin and his repressed associate staring at him wide-eyed from across the table.

Who the hell could have sent it? He glanced around but the sea of women in bathing suits gave him no clue. Jack broke into a sweat that had nothing to do with the sun's burning rays.

"Is it from Lederman?" Mallory asked.

He sure as hell hoped not. "It's personal."

She shrugged. "Okay so do you plan to ask him straight out what's going on?"

He stared over her shoulder, scrutinizing each woman who passed. None gave any indication that they'd sent the note, but *someone* had propositioned him and damn if it didn't sound exciting. Tantalizing. Intriguing.

Hell, he'd be a fool not to show up at eight. And he'd be an even bigger fool to walk into some unknown woman's fantasy.

"Jack? Jack. I asked if you plan to confront Paul Lederman." Mallory asked, obviously confused by his inability to concentrate. She stared at him openly behind those damn black-rimmed glasses.

He had the absurd urge to confide in her and that in itself told him what a bizarre frame of mind he'd been in since starting this trip. Now this. He lifted the note and held it to his nose.

Floral? Oriental? He couldn't place the scent, though he had the sense he'd smelled it before. *In his dreams,* Jack thought.

"Maybe we ought to do this some other time. You're obviously distracted." Mallory rose from her seat.

"Wait."

"Why? Nothing I do or say seems to hold your interest. Why don't you take care of personal matters and we can meet up again later."

He let out a long groan. "Have a seat, Mallory. You asked if I plan on confronting Lederman. The answer is no. This is how the man operates. He likes to build trust slowly. That's why we're here, for him to assess us, to build trust. The firm still handles most of his business, but this…this is personal. When he's ready, he'll confide.''

''And in the meantime?'' She tapped her foot against the white concrete.

''We wait. Enjoy the beach. The view.'' *Come on time. And come hungry.* ''The food,'' he muttered.

''Excuse me?''

He shook his head. She was right. No way in hell could he concentrate on business now—whoever sent this invitation could be watching him. Assessing him. Appraising him. His body shook in reaction.

Mallory grabbed for her pad. ''Maybe you're coming down with something. You've got the chills.''

More like he was burning with anticipation. ''You're right. Let's meet up again later.''

She nodded. ''Get some rest first. How does eight tonight sound?''

He sucked in a breath of ocean air and forced a grin. ''I thought I told you to consider this a semivacation. Take the night off and we'll talk in the morning.''

''Suit yourself.'' She turned and walked away.

He followed the sleek way she moved and the sway of her legs in her sensible sandals. Wasted potential, Jack thought, and it was a pity.

But he couldn't think about Mallory now. He waved the note in the air, savoring the lingering scent and the arousing effect the perfume had on his senses. *All* of his senses, and no doubt that was the intention.

Whoever had sent the invitation meant to stimulate and arouse. Well she'd done a damn good job. So good he couldn't get up from this table yet, and probably not for a long while. At least he'd have time to think about whether or not he'd show up as requested.

Who was he kidding? Jack knew damn well he'd be there. Whoever had gone to the trouble of seeking him out deserved to at least have him respond. In person. And his tingling flesh and burgeoning erection left no doubt he *wanted* to make an appearance as well.

TWILIGHT ENVELOPED the beach as night settled in. With burning anticipation, Jack watched the digital clock in his hotel room inch closer to the hour. He had to hand it to the anonymous sender of that note, she'd managed to set the stage for a seduction and keep him aroused the entire afternoon.

A soft breeze swept in through his open terrace door, traveling off the ocean. And his body throbbed in time to the lapping sound of the waves hitting the shore. His heart pounded frantically inside his chest. Desire flowed fast and furious.

Yet he had no idea who he was about to meet.

Did anonymity heighten the sense of anticipation? The excitement? Mystery was a potent aphrodisiac, that much was certain. The need to know, the desire to act out the fantasy, had him ignoring his self-imposed rules against one-night stands. Whether he'd regret making an appearance later, he didn't know. But right now, nothing could keep him from inhaling that intoxicating scent in person. Nothing could prevent him from arriving on time. And as he locked the hotel door behind him and made his way outside and into the dark night, the frenzied fire, already ignited, burst into a potent, powerful flame.

The resort boasted ten secluded cabins, dotted along the beach. Thanks to the map in his hotel room, Cabin 10 wasn't hard to find, even well-hidden beneath lush foliage. But keeping his cool was difficult and by the time he arrived, he'd actually broken into a sweat.

Jack Latham, the self-proclaimed playboy, the man who thrived on challenges and the women who provided them, was jittery and impatient. And also self-conscious, he admitted as he recalled the instructions he'd committed to memory after one reading.

Following those detailed instructions, he closed his eyes, raised his hand and knocked on the cabin door. In the darkness, sounds became magnified and his knuckles rasping against the door pounded inside him as well. Crickets chirped around him and the breeze rustled the neighboring branches. Seconds passed and then he heard creaking hinges as the door opened.

His stomach churned in anticipation and the urge to look was overwhelming. But the instructions had been clear. If he wanted his desires granted, he had to follow the rules and so he kept his eyes shut tight.

Without warning, a soft hand grabbed his wrist. His breath caught in his throat and his mouth grew dry. He found himself locked in a warm and gentle, yet firm and determined, grip. Not a word was spoken but an insistent pull propelled him ahead, probably inside the cabin.

Jack stepped forward, eyes still closed, pulse still hammering out a rapid beat. He crossed a wide expanse of space until a jerk on his wrist stopped him. The warmth of feminine body heat grew closer. He wasn't sure how he sensed it, but somehow Jack knew *she* stood before him. And then he inhaled, taking in the fragrant scent that had been with him all afternoon. Stirring his senses. Teasing his restraint.

Her hands settled on his shoulders and pushed him downward until he was sitting, enveloped by luxurious cushions and what he thought was soft velvet.

"I have to look at you," he murmured.

He sensed the shake of her head, felt the press of delicate fingertips against his eyelids. *Not yet.* The unspoken words hovered between them.

"You followed the instructions, so now you get your wish. You wanted to see the woman beneath the frigid façade." The words were whisper-soft. Featherlight.

But the husky voice was glaringly familiar—and arousing, as it had been from the first. Still, shock propelled his eyelids open.

He expected to see Mallory Sinclair, Esq. Instead he faced a seductress with curves he'd never dreamed Mallory possessed. Glorious waves of black hair flowed over her shoulders. Perfectly applied makeup accented features he had thought only had potential.

He'd been wrong.

Perfection couldn't be improved upon and if he hadn't been so caught up in what *could be,* he would have seen this Mallory all along. Mallory Sinclair, the sultry beauty.

The woman who'd sent him the invitation and who had an evening of seduction in store.

4

"WHAT'S THE MATTER, JACK? Cat got your tongue?"
Mallory leaned so close he couldn't draw a breath let
alone utter a word in response.

Her fingernails, painted a hot coral shade, trailed a
path from his jaw to the top button on his polo shirt.
Her skin was as soft and alluring as her touch and he
shivered at the brazen assault.

"Or maybe your collar's just too tight for you to
breathe and speak at the same time," she murmured.
With nimble fingers, she released the top button.

He would have inhaled easier if not for her warm
breath on his cheek, the pout of her luscious lips also
in a glossy coral and the intoxicating scent surrounding him. All worked together to arouse. He'd known
going in that seduction was the stranger's intent. He
hadn't known he'd be facing his so-called repressed
colleague and in that respect, Mallory had caught him
off guard.

And Jack didn't like surprises. In court he never
asked a question he didn't know the answer to be-
forehand. Too many attorneys had been tripped up by
assumptions. Too many men had been scammed into
thinking they knew the woman they were involved

with. Jack wouldn't let himself be tripped up or scammed, especially by a woman.

He made his own rules then lived by them. But he'd broken one of those rules when he'd responded to the invitation so he had no one but himself to blame if he found himself at a disadvantage now.

"Maybe you just took me by surprise." He met her gaze, stunned into silence once more by the shocking blue of her eyes, surrounded by incredible waves of black hair.

She nodded. "The frigid façade."

He heard the ice in her tone along with the trace of hurt she couldn't hide, but no way would he ever associate this woman with the word frigid ever again.

"I insulted you."

She inclined her head. Assent or was she assessing him? Before he could decide or even wince at his earlier, poorly chosen phrasing, she spoke.

"Yes, you insulted me. Yet I have to admit that was an interesting description of a woman you barely know." Her words implied she intended to correct not only his erroneous assumption but also the status of their relationship.

Her next move proved him right. She settled herself into the seat cushion beside him, so close he forgot to breathe until he forced himself to focus on his surroundings and not his sexy hostess. With his eyes shut earlier, he'd curled his hands around cushioned softness and he realized now his guess had been right— the sofa was crushed velvet, a taupe and white mix of color that complimented the rest of the interior design. Comfortable for both male and female guests.

She curled her legs Indian-style. His gaze was drawn downward to the soft, shimmery material of her skirt, yellow silk beneath a sheath of sheer organza, then to the delicate wisp of a sandal covering her feet. Coral accented her toenails, just as it did her lips and fingernails.

She played with the skirt until it fell provocatively between her legs, covering yet revealing at the same time. She was toying with him. He knew it and so did she, yet he enjoyed the teasing too much to call her on it.

There were no traces left of the staid, uptight, repressed colleague he'd flown with. "I take it I'm here so you can prove my assumption about you was wrong."

As he spoke, he let his gaze travel upward again. Though the skirt was full, it revealed a narrow waist and he had a sudden desire to lift the flowing material and take a look at those legs he'd noticed this afternoon.

"Dichotomy is interesting, isn't it?" she asked.

Tempt. Torment. Tease. Obviously she wasn't going to answer him directly. He met her gaze, and realized she'd caught him staring. He wouldn't apologize. For one thing he wasn't sorry. And for another, her cheeks flushed a rosy pink beneath the artificial color, telling him he affected her, too.

Jack refused to give up what little power he possessed in this game she'd set up. "Everyone and everything in life has two faces, two sides. Not all of them pleasant."

He'd learned early on that his *loving* mother, his

father's *devoted* wife in public, was a cold, uncaring, cheating female in private. As time marched on, she didn't care who knew the truth and the dichotomy she'd presented merged into a singular unhappy woman. Since then, Jack had become an expert on the two faces of human nature.

Mallory's eyes narrowed, as if she realized his words revealed a part of his soul. He silently cursed. How could he forget this seductive female had a brain like a steel trap and the instincts of a killer shark? That *dichotomy* she'd mentioned. The one he'd always looked for in others. Why did he find it so easy to forget Mallory possessed another colder, more calculating side?

Which Mallory was real, which was the impostor?

"So you're already attuned to the subtleties of human nature. That's good since it makes my job that much easier." She smiled, a sexy smile meant to disarm and make him wonder what she planned next.

He could only wait and see. Despite the danger—to the private emotions she effortlessly tapped into and to the career he'd built and had no business risking for a fling with a colleague—the anticipation stoked a fire of burning need deep inside him. One he didn't fully understand.

Obviously he'd sensed there was more to his repressed colleague than met the eye or he wouldn't have had those occasional bouts of arousal—when he'd heard her husky voice, or inhaled her luscious scent on the plane. The same scent, he now realized, he smelled on the invitation this afternoon. His mind hadn't been ready then to grasp the possibilities. He was ready now. More than ready if the blood pumping through his veins was any indication. She was playing a game and he intended to draw out the intensity and the pleasure.

He had no doubt she'd back off first. The no-office-romance policy would weigh more heavily on her mind since she had a partnership at stake and knew his vote could destroy her chances and all she'd worked for. Not that he'd ever jeopardize her career over this invitation to seduction. He had too much respect for her as a lawyer and too much admiration for the woman who'd lured him here to teach him a well-deserved lesson.

But he could enjoy the steps along the way. "I obviously spoke out of turn this morning by using the word frigid. But the word façade—now that was right on target."

A wide smile touched her face and radiance glowed from the porcelain skin on her cheeks. "You're a smart man, Jack. Façade. Defined it means a false, superficial or artificial appearance or effect."

"And that's what this is?" His hand swept the air around her before he laid his arm back on the couch. Mere inches from the silken bare flesh revealed by the matching camisole she wore.

Though her daily suits did little to reveal womanly curves, Jack saw plenty now. She had full breasts, fuller than he'd imagined and creamy white skin peeked through the deep vee of her top.

"You're wondering which is the real Mallory?" Her sultry laugh lit the night air. "That's for you to find out."

She teased him with what-if's and myriad other sensual possibilities.

"Are you ready to eat?" she asked.

The question led to thoughts of decadent delights, feasting on her glistening lips and tasting her hidden feminine secrets. But he doubted that was what she had in mind.

At least not yet. A wicked voice in his head taunted him, just as her nearness teased him. He wanted to close the distance, to sweep his hand over the expanse of skin on her neck and shoulders, to bring her close enough for him to devour with his mouth.

"I'm hungry," he replied. And if she looked down, she'd see exactly how ravenous he was. He tried to swallow but his throat had grown dry. "But how about a drink first."

She rose from the couch with fluid grace and walked over to the minibar. "Vodka on the rocks, yes?"

He raised an eyebrow. "You remember?"

Mallory nodded. "I pay attention." To everything about you, she thought.

She drank in his charcoal-gray eyes, lit by anticipation and awareness. She took notice of his jet-black hair, combed and sexy despite—or was it because of its perfection? Her gaze dipped lower. The intriguing bit of chest hair visible from his now open collar was seared into her memory.

Jack Latham was a potent masculine package. And that was the problem. Her mental obsession with him and what he thought of her had brought her to a dangerous precipice. He'd challenged her femininity and she'd responded, putting her career and her future on the line. She could not believe she'd taken her humiliation over his insulting comment this far. But now that she had, Mallory had no choice but to follow through with her plan to show Jack *the woman* behind the façade.

"I pay attention, too. Your reputation for thoroughness and your expertise is unrivaled among the firm's associates."

She warmed at his compliment, knowing she'd transformed herself into the frigid Mallory for that very purpose. "Thank you."

After pouring his vodka and her wine for much needed courage, she returned to the sofa. With any luck she could remain in control of herself and her reactions at the same time she tested his.

She handed him his glass and their hands touched. Brief and accidental, yet a tremor of awareness ricocheted throughout her body. So much for control, Mallory thought. Since he was here in response to her invitation and he didn't seem inclined to bolt now that he realized *she* was the invitee, she willed herself to remain calm, forget business and concentrate on Jack.

By the time the evening was over, Jack would have no doubts regarding Mallory's womanly attributes and feminine wiles. Point made, things between them then could return to normal. As if anything could ever be normal again now that she'd come this close to her fantasy.

She seated herself beside him and silence followed. "So tell me about the Terminator," she said, before he could take charge of the conversation.

"It's a great movie but the first was better than the sequel," he said quickly.

Too quickly and his expression grew shuttered as it had earlier, when he'd discussed the two sides of human nature.

She sensed his discomfort and wondered at the cause of his withdrawal. She lifted her drink to her lips and took a long sip.

The fruity liquid slid down her throat, wetting her mouth so she could speak. "I agree. Sequels are rarely as good as the original. In *Terminator Two*, there were too many muscles on Linda Hamilton. Yet she made the men drool." Mallory shrugged. "I always thought men liked their women on the softer side."

Surprise at her response registered on his face. Obviously he thought she'd continue to push him for answers about what made him the office terminator. Her cousin Julia would have taken a more overt approach. Mallory preferred subtlety. She was coming on strong enough as it was.

And this way, he wouldn't know he was easy to read. His poorly timed movie joke had given her a more personal glimpse into his feelings about being the marriage terminator than if he'd answered with dry facts. There was time enough for those.

She ran her tongue over the rim of the glass, savoring every droplet of wine. She was gratified when his gaze followed the movement and his eyes dilated with desire.

His stare locked with hers and though he'd obviously been caught again, he didn't back off or look away. He was as direct as she'd been in bringing him here and she appreciated his forthrightness.

"So what's your take? How do you like your women, Jack? Soft and feminine or harder with an edge of steel?"

A smile lifted the corners of his mouth into a sexy grin. "I like them to possess a bit of both. Strong and capable on the outside, yet soft and pliant, warm and giving within." He reached forward and grasped her glass, easing it out of her fingers and placing it on the table beside the couch.

"Sort of like you," he murmured. He tucked a strand of hair behind her ear.

His touch was warm and sexy, like the timbre of his voice and she reacted. Her nipples tightened beneath the silk and the bare wisp of a bra she wore. Another gentle caress like that last one and she'd lose what little semblance of control she possessed.

He placed his glass beside her own. "Unless of course, this is an act."

Aah. He wanted to test her limits and see if she turned back into uptight, frigid Mallory. He wanted to see who would run first. Poor Jack. He had no idea she was prepared to see this through and deal with the consequences later.

"Maybe it is an act. Maybe it isn't. The point is you still aren't sure, are you?"

"Not yet." He leaned forward until his lips were mere inches from hers. "But the night's still young and I plan to find out."

His mouth hovered close to hers. Hot with a hint

of Absolut vodka, his breath teased her with seductive promises she wasn't ready to make or keep. Yet.

"Not so fast." She playfully pushed back on his shoulders before he could possess her mouth in the kiss she so desperately wanted despite the need to back off. If there was any kissing to be done tonight, she'd be the one to initiate. Otherwise she had no prayer of proving her point. And that's what tonight was all about, she reminded herself. Proving a point not gaining pleasure, though she sensed she'd experience that, too.

But she couldn't risk serious involvement with Jack Latham and anything beyond this playful evening would constitute involvement. Something neither her emotions nor her career could afford.

She'd spent too many years building toward a partnership. Too many lonely, unfulfilled years maybe, but if she was going to receive the ultimate payoff in the end, she couldn't succumb to emotional need or desire with the one man she'd always wanted. Not now. She hoped Jack took her teasing in the right light or she'd ruin everything anyway.

Forcing herself to remember her priorities, which wasn't easy when kissing Jack was within easy reach, she rose from her seat. "You said you were hungry." She walked over to the table where room service had left a full meal including hors d'oeuvres.

"Starved." His deep chuckle reverberated behind her.

He wouldn't be amused by the time she was through.

"I thought you were staying in the main hotel."

She appreciated the switch to mundane conversation. "Keeping tabs on me?"

"If I wasn't before, I will be now." She pivoted toward him in time to see Jack shake his head. "I didn't mean that the way it sounded."

"Sure you did. That's why we're here." She toyed with a tray of grapes and assorted cheeses displayed in an elegant spread. One she'd added her own finishing touches to before Jack had arrived. The only question that remained was whether she had the nerve to carry out her plan.

Frigid façade, frigid façade. His words echoed in her mind and rankled every one of her feminine instincts. He didn't know anything about her and she wanted him to learn.

She didn't ever want him to forget.

"Actually, my secretary made the reservations so I know we're on the same floor. Across the hall, in fact," Jack said.

"These villas are available to rent for special occasions." She set the tray in front of them on a small table and plucked a grape from its mooring.

"And this is a special occasion?" A wry smile formed on his lips.

"If that's your take on the evening, I'm pleased." She popped the fruit between her lips. The succulent juice burst, coating her mouth.

"I notice you don't always answer a question directly."

She edged closer to him. "I'm a lawyer. I'm trained in the technique of evasion."

"It doesn't look like you're evading now," he murmured.

She leaned forward, her weight braced on the palms of her hands. "Do you like grapes?"

He briefly glanced at the tray before meeting her gaze. "I could be persuaded to have a taste."

"I hoped you would say that." Now or never, Mallory thought and closed the distance between them, placing her lips over his.

Jack's eyes registered first surprise, then darkened with desire. Closing her eyes so she wouldn't drown in his gaze, she rubbed her lips delicately over his, using the juice from the grapes to tease and arouse. His lips were damp, tasting of vodka and man as a low groan escaped from the back of his throat. A curling warmth exploded in her belly with the knowledge that her passion was reciprocated. But it wasn't enough.

"You wanted to taste grapes." Her words were muffled against his lips. "Open up and taste the fruit, Jack."

She knew he wasn't a man prone to taking orders yet she didn't have to demand twice. His lips opened on command and she slipped her tongue inside his hot, moist mouth. She'd read somewhere that the salivary glands under the tongue could be stimulated easily and secrete a sweetness that was unbearably arousing. She tested that theory now, using her tongue beneath his, to dart in and back, to tease before finally tangling and twining with his.

His groan came harsher this time and she felt his body shudder in return. His hands came up to brace her cheeks, to tip her head and hold her in place. Her heart beat hard and fast inside her chest along with an accompanying pulsing that had taken up a steady rhythm between her legs. One she felt, too, in the base of her throat.

In all her years, she'd never experienced the flame of desire raging out of control. Though she enjoyed sensuality, she'd yet to find a man who unleashed her hidden self. Jack Latham was that man and the yearning wouldn't be denied. His arms grasped her waist and pulled her closer. Mallory responded, arching her back, deliberately rasping her painfully erect nipples against his chest, seeking relief, seeking him.

She'd set this scenario into motion but she'd only pictured Jack's response to the feminine side he didn't believe existed. Not once had she taken her own reactions into account. Even if she had, she'd never have been able to imagine such pleasure from a mere kiss. Such an all-consuming, building need inside her.

All from taking charge of the feminine desires she'd denied for too long. From letting loose the fantasy she'd always had surrounding this man.

Without warning, his tongue became more demanding, more insistent. He took control with the same sweeping, thrusting movements she'd tried on him. He was persistent, hot and erotic, on her palate, beneath her tongue, taking and draining every bit of moisture she possessed. Was it her imagination or was the sweetness of the wine magnified when shared? She tipped her head back and he swept the deep recesses of her mouth like a lover thrusting into carnal oblivion.

A small voice in her head whispered something about teaching him a lesson and warned her to take back control before it was too late. His lips felt so hard and so right, his touch so demanding she wanted to succumb to every sensation, taste and nuance. By the time he slowed and nibbled on her lower lip, every nerve ending she possessed was on fire. Her every thought and desire was attuned to Jack's.

She reached her hands out to cup his wrists, taking hold of something, anything to keep her grounded. She couldn't say who broke the kiss first, but when they separated, she needed the heated touch his skin provided, needed the connection with him to remain. Not a good sign, Mallory thought, amazed she could think at all.

"Delicious." His low, throaty voice sounded more like a growl.

"So you liked the juice from the grapes." A smile curved her now sensitive lips.

He nodded. She lifted the circular ring of grapes from the tray and draped it provocatively around her neck.

His eyes opened wide but he didn't miss a beat. "I liked them but I think I need another taste to be sure." He dipped his head and nibbled on the necklace she'd created and Mallory thought certain she'd died and gone to heaven before she realized she'd never been that good or deserving in her life. She certainly wasn't being a good girl now.

His dark head bent over her chest and his silky dark hair brushed her throat. He smelled uniquely male and the scent rushed through her body as potent and heady as liquid desire. And his lips—those lips that had accepted her teaching and then kissed her with great skill now grazed not just the fruit, but her flesh. Warm laps of his tongue were followed by shorter, nibbling bites that just happened to miss the grape and end up on her skin.

She shuddered and moaned. She tipped her head back to give him better access. To the succulent fruit or to the waiting cleavage between her breasts. She sighed when his breath teased and groaned but he didn't touch.

When he finally lifted his head, a wicked grin curved his lips.

"Now how were they?" She managed to summon a strong voice, determined to maintain control of the situation despite the fact that she'd never felt less in control of herself or her body.

His darkened gaze remained steady on hers. "Sweet and giving."

Moisture pooled again in her mouth.

"Damp, not dry."

Heat pounded low in her stomach.

"Surprisingly hot to the touch."

Dampness trickled from between her legs yet somehow she managed to form a coherent thought and speak. "Hot?" The word escaped her burning throat.

"Sizzling."

Like the heat that flared in his eyes, Mallory thought. "As in the opposite of frigid?" she asked.

A grin caught hold of his lips. "Most definitely."

With more regret than she'd let him see, she leaned

forward and brushed her lips over his for one last kiss. One last lingering taste before she forced herself to her feet, and rose on unsteady legs.

He leaned back and eyed her warily, though thanks to his analytical mind, Mallory sensed he knew exactly what she was thinking. His next words proved her right.

"You made your point."

"I suppose I did." In more ways than one, she thought, knowing she'd learned a valuable lesson tonight as well.

She inclined her head to one side. Thanks to his indulgent ministrations, the brush of her hair against her shoulders felt like an erotic caress against her sensitized skin.

No way did she want the evening to end, but she'd accomplished her goal and a good strategist got out at the optimum moment—before they lost what they'd gained. "So I guess we can call it a night."

Something flickered in his darkened gaze. She'd like to think it was dismay.

"I suppose so." He rose from his seat. As he began a lazy, sexy stride toward the door, he turned back and approached her once more. "You're one hell of an opponent, Mallory Sinclair."

His lips touched hers too briefly and then he was gone, leaving Mallory alone, sexually charged and for some strange reason she didn't understand, emotionally unfulfilled.

She lifted the ring of grapes and she wondered who had been the teacher and who the student. And who had learned the greatest lesson of all. Because though she'd taught Jack his well-deserved lesson, she now knew she could never repeat the instruction without succumbing herself.

5

JACK ROLLED to his side and came face-to-face with the glare of the morning sun streaming through the windows. The shades he'd forgotten to draw when he'd come in late last night mocked him and reminded him how distracted he'd been upon his return.

The source of that distraction haunted him still.

Mallory. They'd never eaten dinner, the episode with the grapes providing enough sustenance for them both. Though he hadn't quenched the full extent of the hunger she'd inspired, he hadn't forced the issue. Instead he'd let her call an end to the evening and had made his escape while he was still able to think clearly. Before he'd taken things with his colleague too far.

His colleague. He wondered if he'd ever be able to think of Mallory as just his co-worker ever again. A vision of coral—lips, toes and fingers—hovered behind his closed eyes. He could still feel those nails digging into the skin on his wrist as she kissed him into sensual, sexual oblivion. He sat up and swung his legs over the side of the bed. A slight pounding in his head leveled off to a dull roar, a combination of vodka, which he didn't drink often, and shock. He'd known Mallory was his intellectual match and he'd respected her abilities. He hadn't known she was a woman capable of enticing him sexually as well.

But that had been her point—to teach him a lesson about jumping to conclusions and punishing him for his casually tossed insult. Jack had always been a good student and last night he'd learned fast. And now that he'd seen her other side? Now that he'd been exposed to the duality that existed within her, could they go back to a peaceful working relationship?

He shook his head. The barriers she'd always kept in place were gone for good along with the cool pretense. No way did he believe she could or would keep him at arm's length by dressing the part of the repressed attorney any more than he could ignore truth. She was a beautiful woman with a sensuality he longed to explore.

And he wanted to be the man to plumb her hidden depths. Their working relationship be damned.

He glanced at the phone and noticed the blinking red light for the first time. He wondered if he'd slept through a phone call or if he'd managed to miss the message indicator late last night. He dialed the voice mail, an amenity of Lederman's luxury hotel, and listened to the message. His host had canceled all meetings today as he'd unexpectedly been called out of town.

Jack didn't like the man's disappearance any more than the sudden and strange, personal phone calls Lederman had received. More accurately he didn't trust them. Jack never took on a case he didn't feel confident he could win. Not that he won them all, but he had to have faith in the dispute he was fighting.

Before he committed to this case or Lederman committed to him, he had to figure out what the hell the man was hiding.

And he had to fill Mallory in on today's change of plans. A quick shower to clear his head and he'd have no choice but to face his beautiful, no longer repressed colleague. His only consolation lay in the fact that she had to face him as well.

''ANSWER THE PHONE.'' Mallory tapped a pencil against the wooden nightstand in her hotel room and listened to the incessant ringing in her ear. Where was Julia and why wasn't she answering the phone? Leave it to her night-owl cousin to be out at the crack of dawn the one time Mallory needed her advice. Her more worldly advice.

Mallory might enjoy feminine accessories, lingerie and the more sensual touches, but her experience with the opposite sex was lacking. With most of her time spent on her career, she rarely had the opportunity for relationships or the time to devote to the how-to's of snagging a man or keeping his interest. Not that she wanted to maintain Jack's interest, she assured herself. She'd already proved her point and satisfied a fantasy in the process. Time to move on.

But she desperately needed to talk to her cousin, her closest friend since childhood. The one person who could help put last night in perspective for her. Once Julia got past the shock. Mallory's spur-of-the-moment decision regarding Jack had been more out of character than even he realized. She'd astonished herself and could only imagine what he thought of her now.

No one answered on the other end of the phone. Apparently she'd have to rely on herself, something she'd done all her life on the fast career track, so there was no reason why she couldn't trust her judgment now. She hung up the phone and sat up straighter, feeling more confident with the reminder.

Last night she'd had Jack eating out of the palm of her hand, or more accurately off the grapes around her neck, she thought, shivering at the sensual on-slaught of memory. His tongue lapping her skin, his lips moist and warm against her flesh, inches away from the slope of her breast and the rigid, aching nipple. She closed her eyes and allowed the remembered sensation to wash over her before forcing her mind back to today's reality. If she could handle him in the throes of passion, she could certainly handle him over the breakfast table this morning.

Having made her point, things between them could return to normal. She repeated the mantra throughout her morning shower and regular routine, and reiterated the words as she made her way down to the coffee shop inside the hotel where they were sched-uled to meet with Mr. Lederman. At least she'd have the eccentric older man as a buffer between them to break any initial tension.

The hostess walked her to an empty table and she chose the seat facing into the restaurant. With no breathtaking view to look at, no fresh air and ocean breeze blowing through her hair, and neither the tangy scent of salt or the warm coconut fragrance of sunscreen to wreak havoc on her senses and distract her, she should be able to concentrate on business with no problem, Mallory thought.

And then she laid eyes on Jack as he walked into the restaurant.

She thought she'd been prepared. His preppy afternoon outfit yesterday had been charming. His casual choice of clothing last night had been sexy but manageable. But today's choice of royal-blue swim trunks and white athletic tank top revealing deeply bronzed skin threatened to be her undoing, leaving her breathless and speechless at the same time.

Not a good combination for a woman who'd convinced herself she was in control. "Morning, Jack." She pasted on her brightest smile and met his gaze.

"Mallory." His voice was gruff, reminding her of all that had passed between them last night.

He stared at her, eyebrows lifted high, shock registered on his face. She knew without him saying a word, her clothes and hairstyle both surprised and disappointed him. Her choices had been a deliberate part of her plan to return things between them to normal.

But her heart had begun a frantic, pounding beat, one she couldn't calm with slow, deep breaths or a calculated selection of wardrobe. Normal obviously couldn't be achieved by outward appearances alone. Not anymore. She sighed. Yet another sign she'd crossed into scary territory with this man.

Determined to maintain control, she held his gaze, refusing to back down first until he finally averted his stare with a muttered growl. He seated himself, not across the table from her as she'd expected, but close beside her. Too close.

His body heat, greater than the morning sun overhead, put her even more off balance. Only a verbal barb could maintain distance between them now.

She forced a welcoming smile. "I was starting to think I'd have to call out the National Guard to look for you," she said. "Rough night?"

Jack blinked and exerted all the energy he possessed into remaining in his seat and *not* pulling the pins out of her tight bun, or opening a button on her suit jacket to reveal the skin he'd laved so thoroughly last night.

Anger and frustration. He wasn't sure which emotion was stronger but he refused to let her see either.

He shook his napkin out and placed it on his lap. "Nope. I slept fine. You?"

She shrugged. "No problem."

A waitress paused at the table to hand them menus. "Coffee while you're waiting for the third person?" she asked.

"Yes, please," Jack said. "But there's been a change and it's just the two of us for breakfast."

Mallory gasped in surprise and Jack took perverse pleasure in being able to shock her as well.

"I'll give you a few minutes to decide, then." The other woman walked away.

"What happened to Mr. Lederman?" Mallory asked.

"He got called out of town."

"Over the weekend?" she asked incredulously.

"With us waiting here to discuss the possibility of handling his divorce?"

So it sounded strange to her, too. Jack nodded. "Doesn't make sense to me either. We're going to have to figure out what's going on with him."

"Do you think he's having an affair?"

"Good possibility."

"You didn't need to think that one over." A frown turned her lips downward.

He preferred her smiling. "Never discount any angle."

She tipped her head to the side and he imagined her black hair falling over her shoulders in disarray. After last night's revelation, not even the severe bun was a distraction to his hormones.

"After you mentioned his disappearing act in the sauna yesterday, I tried to come up with the one thing he'd hide from his potential attorney. An affair was it. I mean anything else and he'd come clean."

"Possibly. I'll talk to him as soon as he gets back. If we're going to represent him I don't want any surprises. The more we know the more we can prepare for ahead of time."

"Sounds like a good plan. I'll work on getting information on Mrs. Lederman in the meantime. Maybe you could scour the premises or something. There's got to be information waiting to be dug up by an intrepid guy like yourself."

Jack muttered about crazy women, grabbed for the menu and flipped it to the breakfast offerings on the back.

Mallory did the same. As she sat perusing the

choices, Jack wondered if she was as calm inside as she appeared. His ego needed to believe she wasn't finding the cover as easy this morning as it had been in the past.

Last night had convinced him *this* Mallory was the façade, a veneer to cover the real Mallory, the passionate woman beneath the disguise.

"Have you decided?" The waitress returned, interrupting his train of thought.

"Mallory?"

"You go first. I'm not sure yet."

"I'll have the Hungry Person Breakfast." Jack handed the other woman the menu. "I missed dinner last night and I'm starving."

Jack spoke to the waitress, but his gaze never left Mallory and he was rewarded. With his mention of last night, a flush crept up her cheeks, betraying her outward calm.

"Whatever happened to Hungry Man or Hungry Woman?" Mallory asked, an obvious attempt to distract herself and him.

The waitress laughed. "That's Mrs. Lederman's contribution to the menu. She says since women can get as hungry as men there's no reason to offer two choices for the sake of using gender distinction."

Mallory smiled and even behind the thick lenses, her blue eyes sparkled with laughter. "Now there's a woman after my own heart." She handed the waitress her menu. "I'll have the same."

"You got it."

As soon as the other woman disappeared out of

view, Mallory leaned forward, arms braced on the table. "Do you realize what that means?" she asked.

"Mrs. Lederman hides a feminist side?"

"Mrs. Lederman's had some say in hotel business. Granted it's just a breakfast selection, but my gut tells me there's more. Maybe she's so calm about this divorce because not only does she not want it, but because if she's forced into it she knows she's got strong legs to stand on when dividing assets." Mallory leaned back in her seat, folding her arms across her chest. "Maybe Mrs. Lederman's smarter and more on top of things than she's letting on."

Her perception impressed him and he admired her sharp mind at work. "Definitely something worth exploring." He took a sip of his black coffee, needing the rush of caffeine to clear his head and get through this meal with his colleague who'd become much more to him in a very short time.

Last night she'd set out to teach him a lesson and she had. Tonight, he decided, would be his turn. He was a man who worked best on challenge and spur of the moment inspiration. Mallory provided both.

He wasn't through exploring her hidden depths. Not by any stretch of the imagination. "So after breakfast are you interested in joining me for a walk on the beach?"

She glanced down. "I'm hardly dressed for the outdoors."

He recognized the excuse. "But your room's right upstairs."

"I didn't bring any kind of beach clothes." She

averted her gaze and he knew she was attempting to avoid him.

He wanted to smile but held back. Apparently she liked being in control and ran when she wasn't. "There's a shop in the lobby." He pressed his advantage.

"They may not have my size."

This time he did grin. "Okay, Mallory. You've forced my hand. I've learned something about you this trip and you don't like an insult or a challenge. Are you afraid to take that walk on the beach? Does being alone with me scare you?"

She stiffened in her seat and Jack was pleased to realize he'd hit a nerve.

"That's ridiculous," she muttered.

Just then the waitress returned with their meals and Jack waited as she placed their breakfasts down on the table.

"Can I get you anything else?" she asked.

"No thank you," Mallory said.

Jack shook his head.

"Then enjoy." The waitress headed to the next table, leaving them alone once more.

Jack picked up his fork. "Might as well get started." He glanced at his watch. "And plan on joining me on the beach in an hour."

Mallory opened her mouth then shut it again, apparently realizing she'd been had.

He dug into his eggs, knowing he needed all the fortification he could get. Because Jack had learned another lesson last night.

When it came to Mallory, he could expect the unexpected.

MALLORY'S EGGS sat cold on the plate while Jack had devoured his meal. How could she eat when she'd been backed into a corner—a corner, heaven help her, she wanted to be in. But as much as she wanted to be with Jack, she couldn't lose control of herself or the situation.

She was caught between the proverbial rock and a hard place. If she changed into her normal swimwear, the bikini she had hidden in her drawer, she'd not only be giving Jack what he wanted, she'd be ceding control. But he was right and she wouldn't walk away from a challenge, or the plain fact that she wanted this time alone with him.

She placed her napkin on the table. "I'm ready, are you?"

He raised an eyebrow, obviously surprised by her willingness to pick up and go after the roadblocks she'd thrown up earlier. "Don't you want to change?"

She stood and slipped open the button on her jacket, then took the garment off, leaving herself dressed in a camisole. "I'm fine."

He shook his head. "You're a stubborn one, aren't you?"

She shrugged. "It's part of my charm." Leaving him to sign the check, which was a business expense anyway, she headed for the back door to the restaurant leading toward the beach.

No sooner had she opened the door than the fresh

air and saltwater smells assaulted her. She blinked into the bright glare of the sun, focusing on the scene in front of her. Blue water stretched out to the horizon, disappearing into an equally blue sky with barely a cloud and only the sun to disrupt the soft banded hue. Mallory shook her head and took in the beauty. She'd lived in the bustling, congested city for too long. She'd also denied herself the luxury of relaxing vacations on tropical islands and beaches. The tangy scent of the salt, the soft breeze and the incredible view were heaven for her deprived senses.

Jack caught up with her on the sand, completing the perfection of the setting surrounding her. Not that she'd tell him that. She leaned down and slipped off her low pumps and slung them over her shoulder along with her suit jacket, letting her feet luxuriate in the cool, soft sand.

In silence they made their way down to where the water lapped at the shore. Leaving her shoes and jacket on a vacant lounge, she walked side by side with Jack, down the long and empty stretch of beach.

"When's Mr. Lederman due back?" Mallory asked, breaking the silence.

"Sometime this evening is my guess."

"I wonder what his real story is. I know we're missing crucial pieces of information."

A high squeaking noise sounded above them, white seagulls diving through the air, above the water. She glanced back down and caught sight of Jack, taking in his appearance and not caring if he noticed.

He'd shoved his hands into the back pockets of his swimsuit and his powerful legs propelled him along.

She was grateful for the early morning hour and the lack of company joining them on the beach. She wasn't ready to share the man or the moment, she realized, surprising herself.

"Divorce is never easy or honest," he said. "Not between the spouses and not between client and attorney. Most relationships are the same. I ought to know considering I lived it as a child."

"That's so sad." Her mother and father may not have been the best parents she could ask for, but they loved each other and honesty existed between them.

Mallory had never allowed her thoughts to veer in the direction of marriage and family. How could she when her career goals came first and didn't mesh with the concept? That didn't stop her from believing in the institution, though, or the possibility of a real and honest relationship between a man and a woman.

"It's not sad, it's fact."

She shook her head. "No I meant your attitude is sad and so is the fact that you can base it on one kind of life experience. Not all relationships are difficult or based on lies or the divorce statistics would be even higher."

"Maybe they should be. Did you ever consider the fact that many of those who don't divorce merely stay together out of convenience?"

"Did you ever consider the notion that couples stay together out of love and respect for each other and the lives they've built together?" She glanced up at him, suddenly wanting him to view relationships and possibilities as she did.

Not for *them*, she assured herself, because there

was no *them,* but for him. Because he'd be a happier man if his mind and heart could soften toward the idea of honest relationships.

He shook his head. The ocean breeze disheveled his dark hair, blowing strands across his forehead. His laid back, sexy appearance was at odds with the determined, grim look in his eyes.

She supposed his attitude ought to turn her off, but instead she felt more drawn to him than before. A distinct fluttering took up residence in her stomach. She recognized the yearning as sexual desire, the tug at her heart as a more emotional connection.

He'd obviously suffered as a child. So had she. He'd apparently built high walls and defenses. Glancing down at her linen skirt and camisole, she realized she'd done the same. They had more in common than she'd ever believed. His effect on her had always been potent but instead of quenching her desire, last night's sensual give-and-take combined with this morning's beach walk had whet her appetite for more.

More of Jack Latham.

More about Jack.

"I never would have pegged you for an optimist or a dreamer," he said at last.

She smiled. "I hadn't thought of myself in those terms either. If asked I'd have called myself a realist." But apparently a romantic lurked beneath the illusion she'd spent years creating.

"The woman I met last night was no hard-edged realist." His voice took on a gruff edge.

At the reminder of their sensual evening, her body softened and warmed, much the way her mind and heart had already thawed toward Jack. Mallory wondered what would happen if she freed the dreamer inside herself, the one he was obviously drawn to, at least for the nonbusiness parts of this trip. Could she still rein it back in when this excursion ended?

She shook her head, letting the breeze push fallen strands of hair back from her face. Even if she desired more, she couldn't risk her job nor could she potentially risk her heart. She inhaled the salty air, regret infusing her deep inside.

Mallory decided the time for revelations and intimacy had ended. Back to safety. "The woman last night may not have struck you as a realist but the attorney who's helping you on this case is definitely one."

"Return to business." Disappointment flickered in his eyes and laced his tone.

She nodded, knowing she had no choice. "So will you confront Lederman about your suspicions?"

"I was thinking of a more behind-the-scenes quest for information. Whatever you and I can find out before we hit Paul up for details. If our imaginations are acting overtime and he's truly involved with his son and a business deal, then accusing him of an affair or hiding something more will force him into giving the case to another firm."

"Something neither of us want."

"Because you view this as your stepping stone to partnership?" he asked with uncanny accuracy.

"Because the firm has my loyalty, and yes because I want to make partner." And she didn't want her obsession with Jack or her blatant move last night to jeopardize all she'd worked for.

He stopped walking without warning. She didn't realize he wasn't beside her until he called her name. She turned, making her way the few steps back toward him.

"What is it?" she asked.

"I don't want you to think I'd do or say anything to destroy your chances for partnership."

"I'd hope you wouldn't. In fact I guess a part of me must have trusted you not to betray last night or else I'd have been a fool to set that plan in motion."

He reached a hand up to cup her cheek. His warm yet roughened palm caressed her skin. "You're no fool."

The cool breeze blew around them and she shivered, a blatant reaction to his touch and not the ocean air. "Neither are you."

"True. And considering I didn't walk out as soon as I realized it was you, I suppose we're trusting each other not to reveal the fact that we're breaking the no-office-romance rule."

Present tense. Was he asking for more time or was she reading her wishes into his words?

Mallory tipped her head to the side, causing his hand to cradle her cheek in a gentle caress. "Are you telling me Jack Latham is trusting a woman?" she asked wryly.

He grinned. "Trust is easier to give when it's mutual and both parties have something at stake."

"At which point it isn't trust but more like a level playing field."

He burst out laughing. "I really do admire you," he said, sobering. His eyes darkened with desire.

Her heart thudded hard in her chest. "Same here." And she wanted him, with an intensity that frightened her.

To give in to her fantasies again, in daylight no less, would make them that much harder to put behind her when this trip was over. Mallory the dreamer didn't mind.

Mallory the realist knew better than to cross a boundary with no safety net. And that safety net was distance and control.

6

THE TIDE STILL LAPPED at his feet as Mallory looked up at him with wide eyes. Yes, Jack admired her, but did she realize how much he wanted her as well? He could lean forward for a kiss. He could taste the salt on her lips and let her soft body mold against his harder one, but it wouldn't be enough.

And from the hesitant look in her eyes, she wouldn't be receptive. Jack admired her gutsiness and intelligence, her spunk and positive outlook for the future. No matter how strong she'd come on last night, he respected her uncertainty now.

He'd been wrong to think the woman from last night was the real Mallory. In reality she was a fascinating mixture of two personas and she intrigued him on too many levels beyond sexual. The knowledge set off warning bells in his cynical brain.

His encounters with the opposite sex were supposed to be simple and fun. Easy to walk away from, no strings attached, no emotional commitments. But the yearning he felt for Mallory was beginning to surpass mere sexual desire.

He wanted her.

He desired her company, too.

But he yearned for another invitation most of all.

He could see from the determined look in her eyes one wouldn't be forthcoming.

Yet she'd set a challenge in motion last night. She'd proven both her femininity and his susceptibility to her charms. His turn next and he intended to prove she wasn't any more immune to him than he was to her. Up the stakes, even the playing field and they could both retreat, egos intact. Next time.

Kissing her now would destroy any prayer of catching her off guard later. So he pulled back instead. "Ready to go inside?" he asked.

She blinked, obviously surprised at his about-face. He didn't mind putting her off balance for once. She'd done it to him too often.

She shook her head. "You go on. I think I'll hang out here for a while. At least until the sun gets too hot."

They'd each backed into neutral corners. Without her explaining, Jack understood exactly what was going through that analytical brain. The dichotomy in her personality was most evident in broad daylight and there were consequences to *them* she wasn't ready to face.

Kissing under the morning sun would have meant acknowledging she'd crossed the line from proving a point last night to something more between them today. He agreed.

Disappointment churned in his gut but he accepted the parameters. It was the only way he had a chance of seeing Mallory, the sexy seductress, again. "Be careful not to get burned," he said.

A flicker of dismay crossed her features and darkened her blue eyes. Well that was something, Jack thought as he walked away.

The desire to turn back was strong yet he acknowledged their separating now was for the best. He wasn't ready to walk back to their rooms and part in the hall, not when he'd rather take her into his room and then to his bed. Though his mind accepted the need to leave, his body wasn't nearly as understanding and a throbbing, unfulfilled desire remained.

He left her standing on the beach. The image of the wind blowing her tight bun out of order and place, of her wide blue eyes staring at him as he backed off, was etched in his memory. He feared it could make its way to his heart, if he wasn't careful.

But when it came to women Jack was always careful, and Mallory was no exception. He couldn't allow her to become more to him than a private fling. A memory he could cherish and hold on to, but one he could never reveal—not to anyone back home and not even to himself.

He picked up his pace. Was it his imagination or could he feel her burning stare sear into his back as he retreated to the hotel? He shook his head and let himself in through the back door of the restaurant— the fastest way off the beach and out of her line of vision. Away from his own fanciful musings.

Jack passed through the dining area and then the front desk. He rounded the corner to the elevators, pausing by the gym on his way.

He'd been impressed with the facilities when Lederman had taken him on a hotel tour before their sauna. The spa sported a full-service gym with instructors available for a wide range of requests, including a new full cardiovascular workout—under a doctor's supervision.

Jack peered through the glass window to the nearly empty gym. There was no better way to alleviate stress and strain than to work up a good sweat, and no better means of obtaining information than to make conversation with hotel employees. Both would hopefully take his thoughts and desires off Mallory and center them on work where they belonged.

He signed in and grabbed a white towel from the stack behind the registration desk.

"Can I help you?" A dark-haired woman with muscles he'd be proud to possess walked over.

He hung the towel around his neck. "I just thought I'd give the treadmill a run."

She nodded. "No problem. Let me familiarize you with the equipment and you can get started. I'm Eva." She extended her hand. "I'm the manager."

He shook her iron grip. "Jack Latham."

Her eyes widened with recognition. "Nice to meet you. Paul…I mean, Mr. Lederman mentioned you were one of his special guests."

Jack didn't miss the familiarity in her tone when she spoke of Paul Lederman, but he let it slide. He laughed and brushed off her words with a sweep of his hand. "That's Paul for you. But I'm not looking for any special treatment."

She shook her head and her ponytail swished against one shoulder. "Are you trying to cost me my job?" she asked, laughter in her eyes.

"I can't imagine Paul firing you."

"Me neither." She met his gaze with what he could only call a certain yet knowing stare. She was an attractive young woman with curves in all the right places and by her posture and confidence, she obviously knew it.

Silence stretched for a moment in which Jack questioned her relationship with his potential client, then reprimanded himself for looking for fires where there were none. "You always do what the boss says?" he asked.

She glanced away without meeting his gaze. "He pays the bills."

And Jack wondered if he'd hit paydirt. "I'll bet he wishes all his employees were as loyal as you."

"He's a man that inspires loyalty, but being that special guest of his I'm sure you know that. Now let's get you started on that workout." She gestured toward the treadmill.

Jack doubted Paul would have an affair with a woman who worked in the same place his wife lived. Lederman was arrogant to the extreme but he wasn't careless. Not where his empire was at stake. His disappearances were more telling than a young girl's infatuation and if there was a mistress to be found, she wasn't on the premises.

But Jack had a hunch Paul had done nothing to discourage this employee's interest. Her husband's flirting, if that was what had happened, couldn't please Mrs. Lederman. And careless trifling with female employees could be evidence of the man's willingness to take greater risks.

Jack smiled at the pretty manager. "This is one impressive setup you've got here."

"It certainly is. I'm lucky to work in a place like this, but as you probably know there's a story behind it."

Jack didn't know but he sure as hell wanted to find out. "You can say that again. But I didn't realize Paul had begun working out."

Eva nodded. "He starts on the treadmill, too."

"I bet I could benefit from his routine."

She looked him over approvingly. "Oh, it looks like you do just fine on your own."

He hung his towel over a chair and climbed onto the exercise machine. He pressed in the buttons on the computerized equipment and started an easy run.

She watched him, hands on her hips. "Seems like you know your way around these machines. Unlike Paul. You should hear about the first session I ever gave him."

Jack laughed. He'd be more than happy to hear about any session between his potential client and this obviously sensual woman. "I'm not going anywhere so go right ahead."

MALLORY MADE her way from the beach. Sand clung to the soles of her feet and she rinsed them off beneath a minishower before slipping back into her sensible shoes and lifting her sensible jacket off the railing. She sighed, wondering when the trappings of conventionality had become so obvious and constraining.

It was this trip, she thought, feeling every bit of

remaining grit rubbing against her feet as she walked. And it was Jack. Around Jack she wanted to be a sexy, desirable woman so she could watch arousal flare in his dark eyes and know the heat was meant for her alone.

Instead she found herself dressed in garments that were supposed to make her feel an equal in the business world and she'd never felt less womanly or desirable in her life. In fact she felt trapped between the two Mallorys and like Jack, she didn't know which one was real and which one was the impostor.

She slung her suit jacket over one arm but thanks to the salty air and the growing heat, the material stuck uncomfortably to her skin. She took two steps and decided she couldn't take the stabbing pain any longer. Giving up, she pulled off her shoes, hoping she could make it through the lobby and into the elevators unnoticed.

She never made it past the front desk.

"Good morning, Ms. Sinclair."

Startled, Mallory turned to find Mrs. Lederman walking toward her. "I see you've found the beach already this fine day."

Mallory slid a self-conscious hand to her hair. "Is it the wind-blown mess or the scent of the ocean that gave me away?"

The other woman laughed. "Actually it's the trail of sand."

Mallory glanced down to see the traces of sand she'd left behind with each step she'd taken. She sighed, feeling the heat of a flush rise to her cheeks.

"I guess you could say I wasn't dressed for a stroll on the beach."

"Not a problem. We've got kids running through here barefoot all day. This is a resort not a palace. I hope you're finding it to your liking?" The older woman's gaze never left Mallory's face, making her feel as if she were truly interested in her comfort and happiness.

Despite the woman's elegant appearance, she possessed a distinct charm along with motherly instincts Mallory couldn't help but admire. Her own mother had never been as kind or caring. When Mallory had tracked dirt into the house as a child, she found herself with a broom in her hand and facing a disgruntled look on her mother's face. And when she'd annoyed her mother, her father's displeasure was sure to follow.

She glanced at Mrs. Lederman. This woman had every reason to dislike her and treat her with callous disdain, yet not a cruel word or gesture had escaped her perfectly lined and coated lips. Mallory didn't appreciate the painful memories of her childhood this woman evoked, nor did she enjoy the resurgence of longing in her heart. A yearning for acceptance she'd thought she'd banished long ago.

But how could she banish the desire to be loved and accepted when every move in her life had been calculated to gain her parents' respect and admiration, she thought to herself. Their love was a moot point. They reserved that emotion for each other alone.

"Is everything all right?" Mrs. Lederman asked.

Mallory forced a smile as she met the other

woman's compassionate gaze. "As a matter of fact, everything's perfect. Not only is this place beautiful..." Mallory gestured around the contemporary lobby "...but it's a chance to get away from the real world for a while."

"Lucky you. Unfortunately, this *is* my reality." Mrs. Lederman's lips trembled before she was able to hide the signs of her distress.

"Mrs. Lederman..."

She shook her head. "Alicia."

"Alicia." Mallory bit the inside of her cheek. "This is awkward." And though she hadn't approached Alicia Lederman, hadn't been hired and therefore hadn't breached any ethics, Mallory felt uncomfortable.

"Nonsense." Alicia waved a hand in the air, revealing a large solitaire diamond glittering on her left hand.

Obviously Mrs. Lederman hadn't removed her wedding ring. Because she was holding out hope or because she wanted to hang on to the stone? Mallory immediately discounted the mercenary thought. Her instincts were rarely wrong and this woman with warm brown eyes radiated sincerity and goodness.

Kindness that brought back disturbing recollections and led to reinforced insecurities, none of which helped when Mallory had a job to do. Which was to prove to Mr. Lederman she and Jack were the divorce attorneys he wanted on his side.

"It's only awkward if we choose to make it that way," the other woman assured her. "Now is there anything I can do to make your stay more comfortable?''

"Aside from you not being difficult about the divorce or settlement?'' To her credit, Mrs. Lederman didn't flinch, though Mallory did. And inside, her heart died a bit at her own harsh words.

She might have told Jack she'd do whatever it took to make her case, she might even have tried to believe it herself, but she didn't have to like it. And the more she saw of her client's wife, the worse she felt about herself and the side she'd chosen.

Mrs. Lederman drew herself up and squared her shoulders. "You know, I respect the fact that you don't mince words. You remind me of my daughter.''

Mallory shook her head, unable to believe what she'd done. "I'm sorry.''

Mrs. Lederman shook her head. "For being a professional? Nonsense. There's nothing to forgive.''

"Why are you doing this?'' Mallory asked, unable to help herself. "Why are you being so nice to me?''

"Would you believe me if I said I like all guests to enjoy our hotel?''

Mallory nodded slowly. "Yes, I would.'' She'd believe anything Mrs. Lederman said. "Your daughter's lucky to have you.'' The words escaped before Mallory could stop them.

"I wish my husband felt the same.''

That fast, Mallory felt a connection with this woman. One she couldn't afford and one that conflicted with her ultimate aspiration—partnership by virtue of winning Lederman's divorce account for the firm.

From the moment she'd been summoned to Jack's office and placed on this case, she'd known nothing would be easy or simple but she'd never anticipated the turmoil she'd experience here.

Before either of them could say another word, the older woman reached for Mallory's arm and she found herself led across the lobby, around the corner and toward a huge bank of windows. The gym area spread wide in front of her and it was newer and larger than the gym she belonged to at home.

"Nice," she murmured. She leaned closer to the plate glass and saw the room was empty except for a man on a treadmill in the corner.

Make that Jack on a treadmill in the corner with a sexy brunette hanging all over him as he ran. Mallory frowned. Why wasn't the woman repulsed by the smell of sweat? she thought, knowing she was feeling jealous and hating it at the same time.

"Isn't that your colleague?"

Mallory nodded.

"That's our manager," Mrs. Lederman said in response to her unspoken question.

"A little too perfect-looking for my taste," Mallory muttered.

The woman by her side burst into laughter. "Like I said, bluntness becomes you."

Mallory rolled her eyes. "Well let's face it, how many of us actually look like that."

"Not nearly enough and as a man ages, he starts to appreciate youth and well-toned muscles."

Mallory met the other woman's hurt gaze. "Your husband?"

A shuttered look closed Mrs. Lederman's emotions from view. "I thought we were talking about him." A well-manicured fingernail pointed toward Jack.

Mallory narrowed her gaze and looked closer, taking Mrs. Lederman's words into consideration. Yes, this muscled woman was hanging on Jack's every word. And yes, she was taking in his hard calves and thighs and drooling, just as Mallory was. But the key to this scene lay in the visuals or lack of them.

Jack wasn't drooling back. Not that a man could do much obvious ogling of a woman while working out, but his run was paced and he could express more blatant interest if he chose. Even from this distance, Mallory could see Jack's interest lay more in what the woman was saying than what she looked like or wore. In fact, the brunette hadn't stopped talking once since Mallory had begun her watch.

Considering Mrs. Lederman's sudden change of attitude, Mallory believed her husband had caused her jaded views on men and younger, buffer women. And though Mallory hardly thought Jack was undergoing a hardship with this woman's attention, she hoped at least he was getting information on Mr. Lederman from the hard-bodied female ogler.

If any ogling was going to be done over Jack's body, Mallory wanted to do the honors—and she wanted him to eye her right back—as if he couldn't get enough of her. Neither scenario was destined to happen again.

Mallory let out a deep breath. "How about you show me the sauna and whirlpool?" she suggested.

"It's obvious neither one of us want to watch this display."

"Sounds like a good plan. Did I mention we have a masseuse on staff?"

Mallory allowed Mrs. Lederman to lead her on an extended tour, but her mind remained on Jack—who glanced up in time to see her watching him through the large windows.

He proffered a wave, then turned his attention to more shallow pursuits.

JACK LET HIMSELF inside his room. Sweating from his run in the gym, the blast of air-conditioning hit him hard. He raised the temperature dial and sprawled onto the bed.

Today's revelations had wiped him out far more than the workout. Apparently Lederman was having a midlife crisis courtesy of a mild heart attack he'd hidden from all business associates, his attorneys included. According to Eva, the boss's health scare explained the gym's new cardiovascular workouts and doctor on premises and his new dedication to fitness that hadn't yet shown overt results. But the man had started paying more attention to his looks and flirting with the help.

Jack figured it wasn't a far leap to assume the man was fooling around outside his marriage to assure himself of his virility and ability. If so, his attorneys, even potential attorneys, shouldn't be kept in the dark until the bombshell exploded and it was too late to prepare. An affair was the last complication Jack had come here expecting to deal with.

His own or Lederman's.

Jack leaned back and clasped his hands behind his head. Not that an affair was a bad thing—if you were single. And Jack was. Single and primed, by the last woman he'd ever expected.

She haunted his thoughts now, day and night. Even when Eva the spa bunny had outright propositioned him, Jack hadn't been interested. Only one woman held him in thrall.

But apparently Mallory didn't want to continue their…what could he call last night? Liaison? She didn't want to continue their liaison into daylight hours. And with no invitation forthcoming this morning, she obviously had no intention of repeating the episode this evening either.

A one-time lesson. A one-night stand.

On both an intellectual and professional level her decision and withdrawal made sense. But on an emotional plane he didn't comprehend and a sexual one he understood only too well, the frustration and disappointment were overwhelming.

No way would he leave things as unbalanced and unfinished between them as they were now.

7

MALLORY GRIPPED the telephone receiver and waited for the answering machine in her apartment back home to pick up. At the sound of the tone, Mallory yelled into the phone. "Julia, you pick up the phone or so help me when I get home I'll hide all the Godiva chocolate in the apartment. I'll make sure you're banned from Epicurean Delights. I'll…"

The sound of someone fumbling with the phone echoed in her ear, then her cousin's voice. "I was napping and you don't have to get hostile, Mallory Jane."

"Don't call me that." Only her mother called her by her first and middle name, and it had a cold, grating sound Mallory hated, along with memories she despised even more. But as much as Julia thought she knew about Mallory, Mallory had never confided too much. It was almost as if she was counting on making partner to wipe out all the pain in her life.

The rational part of her knew it could never happen. The dreamer Jack had mentioned earlier, well that Mallory clung to the impossible hope. Maybe Jack knew her better than even she realized.

"Mallory? I'm really sorry about that name thing.

It's just that you threatened to deprive me of chocolate and…I lost it.''

"And I overreacted. Where have you been?''

"Here and there.'' Mallory heard the sound of Julia flopping into a beanbag chair and then her cousin spoke. "What's up with you and this Jack person?''

"If I tell you, will you fill me in on what's going on in your life when I get back? Because I can always tell when you're hiding something.'' And Julia had been especially vague about her personal life lately.

"Sure. Sure.''

Mallory sighed. "Why did that sound more placating than convincing?''

"Bad connection? Your imagination? You choose. Now spill.''

"When I get home, Julia Rose.'' Her cousin didn't mind her middle name near as much as Mallory resented hers.

Silence followed. Confident her cousin understood she wouldn't be put off much longer, Mallory felt more comfortable unloading her problems now and taking care of her cousin's in person. "Do you think it's the forbidden that makes him so attractive?''

Her attraction to Jack was more than superficial, but as long as she was in control of her emotions and the situation, she'd be fine. No need to alert Julia of the intensity of those feelings.

Julia exhaled hard. "You know there's no explanation for chemistry. Why are you looking for one?''

"Because nothing about us makes sense.''

"There's an *us?*'' Her cousin's voice pitched in excitement.

Just the thought of an us, of a Jack and Mallory, caused tremors of awareness to ripple through her. Mallory pulled her knees up and tucking the phone between her shoulder and ear, she hugged her arms around her legs for comfort. "No, no us. But there was one night."

And oh, what a night it was. Mallory bit down on her lower lip.

"Ooh, that's not like you. Tell me more."

"That's the problem. It's not like me and now I can't forget about him. Maybe because I...we never actually...well you know, but..."

A loud knock interrupted her unburdening herself. "Gotta go, Julia. Thanks for listening and I'll get back to you," she said to her cousin. "Coming," she called toward the door.

"You can't leave me hanging," Julia wailed.

Mallory chuckled and lightly replaced the receiver. "I just did."

She headed for the door and opened it, chain still latched. When she didn't see anyone, she glanced down and picked up a bag sporting the name of the lobby boutique she'd passed earlier in the day.

Jack. Gut instinct kicked in and her heart pounded out a thready, erratic beat. She had no doubt this wasn't a mistaken delivery and she tore into the bag with a keen sense of anticipation, pulling out a one-piece bathing suit, or a maillot as the label called it.

"French," she murmured aloud.

She fingered the sheer black floral lined in nude fabric. With a high neck and equally high cut-outs up the thighs, the suit was the paradigm of modesty—

and yet it was the sexiest garment Mallory had ever seen.

The note came next and she slit open the sealed envelope and pulled out the white paper with stark male writing. *Suit up and meet me at the beach after dark. I dare you.*

He didn't mention where on the beach but deep in her soul, she knew he meant the place they'd walked earlier. A shudder shook her, one having nothing to do with the cool air-conditioning in the room. Her nipples puckered and her knees buckled. God the man was good.

Instead of just an invitation, he issued a challenge. A subtle one to be sure, but without the *I dare you* line, Mallory would have felt free to ignore the request. The desire to show up in this magnificent suit would have been overwhelming, but common sense could have won out. Common sense was nowhere to be found now. Thanks to the phrasing of the note.

And he knew it.

Obviously Jack had given thought to this evening and to the exact words that would both intrigue her and dare her to resist. Even if his motives were selfish or a bit egotistical—and she didn't doubt he wanted to prove *she* could succumb to his charms the same way he'd succumbed to hers—he'd given thought to what made Mallory Sinclair tick.

Who else in her life had ever done such a thing? Not her parents who knew one another inside and out but barely knew their own child, and not the occasional men she'd dated who wanted a good time or an introduction into the Waldorf, Haynes's world. For this brief interlude of time, Jack's motives didn't matter.

His actions did.

She walked over to the mirrored closet and shrugged out of the terry hotel-styled robe, leaving herself dressed in nothing but lace panties and a sheer bra. She held the sexy bathing suit in front of her. The black suit picked up the inky coloring of her hair and thanks to the contrast, her pale skin took on a porcelain glow.

Or was it the excitement of the challenge that lit her eyes, and the sheen of anticipation and sexual awareness that shimmered in her face?

So he wanted to one-up her, did he? Issue an invitation of his own? Mallory slipped out of her bra and panties, replacing the sheer garments with the seductive suit.

She'd accept his challenge and beat him at his own game.

As THE SUN BEGAN TO SET, an orange haze settled where the water met the sky. Jack watched the sunset with anticipation and as darkness fell he glanced back toward the wooden stairs leading from the hotel to the beach and was struck by the incredible beauty of the woman walking toward him.

He'd chosen the stretch of beach they'd walked on this morning, knowing she'd innately return to find him here based on his note. He'd also walked this area at night and knew it was rarely traveled by guests. Then he'd chosen her bathing suit on a whim, having no idea how it would look on Mallory's supple curves. His only criteria had been sleek, sexy and enough coverage to make her comfortable yet still make him hot.

He'd more than accomplished his goal.

She came toward him with long-legged strides, confident in both her appearance as well as her effect on him. He could tell by the sultry swing of her hips and the smile on her face—it might be *his* invitation but she planned to take control. How very surprised she'd be.

"Glad you could make it." He rose from his seat on a large beach blanket he'd bought for the occasion.

"Did you doubt I'd come?" Her sexy smile grew wider.

"Not for a minute." His words of challenge had been phrased to ensure her arrival. But he realized now he wanted her here willingly and not under duress. Not because she couldn't resist a dare, but because she couldn't resist him.

She shook her head. That gorgeous mane of hair she hid during the day fell over her shoulders in windblown disarray. "Am I really that predictable?"

He reached out and lifted a strand of hair, curling it around his finger. "You're lots of things but predictable isn't one of them."

He met and held her gaze for an intense instant, then he unwound his finger from her hair and glanced back toward the ocean, trying to assimilate the feelings rioting through him that had begun to cross the boundary beyond sexual.

When he glanced back, she'd bent to pull a pair of delicate sandals off her feet and he caught an enticing view of cleavage inside the so-called modest bathing suit he'd chosen.

She tilted her head and met his gaze. "Hey put those eyes back in your head. I'm here to swim only." Rising, she tossed her shoes onto the sand beside the blanket.

"That's too bad. And here I thought you were going to give skinny-dipping a try." He shoved his hands into the back pocket of his shorts to prevent himself from reaching for her, stripping her of that bathing suit and living out the fantasy. Just the two of them with miles of ocean and no clothes in sight.

She laughed. "Very funny."

He didn't think so, and at this moment, neither did his groin, which was straining uncomfortably against his shorts.

She wiggled her toes. He watched as she dug those coral painted toenails into the cool sand and stifled a groan. He had no doubt she was torturing him on purpose.

"Have you ever?" she asked.

"Ever what?"

"Ever gone skinny-dipping?"

He couldn't believe they were having this conversation. Not while she stood inches away, breasts straining against the nearly sheer fabric, tempting him with hidden secrets she had yet to reveal.

"Tell you what. I'll break the ice. I've gone skinny-dipping." She clasped her hands behind her back, rocked on her heels and grinned.

He raised his eyebrows in surprise. Damn but she had a way of catching him off guard. He supposed a part of him still thought of her as prim and proper Mallory because she'd actually shocked him with the admission.

He shut his eyes against the carnal images she provoked deliberately. "Let me guess. Kiddie pool at day camp."

She laughed, the sound breaking through the night air and the crashing waves behind them. "Not hardly. High school, senior year. Prom night. My last hurrah."

Mallory recalled her one and only venture into the waters nude—like tonight it had also been on a dare. She'd grasped at that one last bit of spontaneity and freedom before buckling down for her ordinary, well-planned life.

"Did you like it?" A grin caught his lips in a devastating smile.

"Not as much as I'd thought I would." As she listened to the sound of the water around them, she recalled the chillier waters on a cool May night at the New Jersey shore. A stark difference from the warmer summer waters here. "Let's just say it was an experience."

He shook his head, a combination of amusement and amazement lighting his expression. "If I hadn't seen you in action last night, I'd never believe you had it in you."

"There's a lot you don't know about me." And she was surprised she'd divulged as much as she had.

Even Julia didn't know she'd shed her good-girl inhibitions that one night. But Mallory was learning that Jack was a surprisingly easy man to open up to, and she enjoyed the intimacy created by revealing her secrets under the night sky.

His eyes focused on her, intent and serious. "Good thing I'm an eager student. I want to learn all about you." He held out his hand. "Walk with me."

She accepted the gesture. Warm and eager, his fingers closed around hers and he tugged her toward the rushing tide. Cool water lapped at her bare feet in erotic contrast to the heat inside her.

"You never answered the question. Skinny-dipping," she reminded him. "I've done it. Have you?" She dared a glance from the corner of her eye.

"Would you respect me in the morning if I said no?" He bowed his head at the admission.

Jack Latham, embarrassed? Her heart skipped a beat at his surprising confession. The exchange of secrets had just become mutual. Her body hummed in keen anticipation of more closeness to come, so she didn't make light of his honest statement.

"I respect the truth. So why wouldn't I respect you?" She opted for sincerity since heckling him now would only drive him away and she wanted him as close as he could get. "How'd you miss out?"

He shrugged. "No opportunity. We grew up in the city. I've been sprayed by many a fire hydrant but I've never dipped."

"You never left the city? Not on a vacation or anything?"

"We didn't do family vacations."

Her chest constricted at the unsaid but implied discontent in his childhood. "Neither did we," she admitted softly.

She caught the flicker of recognition in his eyes, of a possible kindred spirit who understood.

"There's always time." She deliberately downplayed the subject. Only she needed to know he'd given her ammunition for a more opportune time. Another night, another invitation.

He paused and pulled her close beside him. "How about now?"

She shook her head. He was naughty tonight and she liked his playful side. "How about not? I like to wade before diving in. Test the waters, you know?"

Those intense eyes seemed to darken even more. "Why do I get the sense you're testing me?"

"Because we're obviously alike. Neither of us can resist a challenge."

His hands grasped her hips as he drew her against his hard body. He held her in place, letting her feel the pressure of his erection, stiff and unyielding against her stomach. She steeled herself against the waves of longing inside her, but they came hard, stronger and more insistent than the crashing of swells lapping at her feet.

"Is a challenge the only reason you're here?" he asked.

A snappy retort sprung to mind, but she squelched it. The challenge may have given her the excuse to accept the invitation but she was here for many more reasons than a dare.

She glanced up at him. "I'm here because you invited me."

"That I did." A teasing glint lit his gaze, but behind the dark depths Mallory saw deeper emotion, a yearning she couldn't name, but one she understood because it existed inside her, too, in a place no one saw and especially not in daylight.

But it was nighttime now and she felt free to indulge her desires—and Jack's as well. He smiled and deep grooves etched the corners of his mouth, dimples she hadn't realized he possessed.

Mallory didn't know what overcame her, but she leaned forward, inhaling the scent of salt water and pure man before she touched her lips to first one dimple, then the next, pausing only to dart her tongue into the intriguing crevice of the stubble-roughened skin of his cheek.

His reaction was a purely masculine groan, one that reverberated inside her and set off an explosive, toe-curling burst of arousal.

"Do you have any idea how hot you make me?" His grip on her waist tightened and his hips jerked forward in an instinctive motion.

He was hard and masculine and felt oh, so good. She sucked in an unsteady breath. "I can feel that I do."

His hands came farther around her back until his palms rested firmly on her behind. She felt herself straining against him, seeking deeper contact than their bodies and positions allowed.

"Relax." His warm breath blew into her ear. The erotic wisp of air tickled her neck and the excitement caused her nipples to tighten and pucker beneath the constraints of her bathing suit.

He held her in place, his hands gently stroking her behind until her lower body, strung tight, did as he asked. She relaxed and molded to him, fitting herself snugly into his erection.

"Much better." His hips swayed seductively against hers. With each rocking motion, a wave of tormenting desire shook her. And with each surge came the ridiculous hope that like herself, he was here with her for more than just a dare.

It had to be the magical, mystical moonlight that allowed her to even consider such foolishness. They were lawyers in the same firm, both thriving on competition and one-upmanship. They had that much in common, yet they had no possible future no matter how hot the chemistry.

They were co-conspirators in this seductive game and that diminished the risk and leveled the playing field. At least, she hoped. There was no denying that with this invitation they'd reached the point of no return. She had no choice now but to believe in his integrity, knowing her career was in his hands. There was no turning back.

Not in the midst of this heated game. And it was hot. With deliberate precision, she mimicked his movements, placing her hands on his backside and pressing him more firmly, more intimately against her. His deep groan of satisfaction caused a trickling of damp desire to settle between her legs. The hard planes of his chest brushed against her aching breasts and relief seemed so close yet so very far away.

IT WAS HOT, Jack thought, this wicked fling beneath the moonlight that mimicked hot sex yet fell short of mutual satisfaction. He didn't know how much longer he could rock against her willing body yet get no relief against the crescendo of need building inside him.

He'd meant to give her sweet torment and take her further than she'd taken him last night, but she'd turned the tables, torturing him instead, and imminent release was building fast and furious inside him.

At least he wouldn't be alone if he took that plunge, but it wasn't the ending to the night he'd originally envisioned. He had no intention of embarrassing either of them when all he wanted was to take her to the edge and give her a night to remember.

Without speaking, he swept her into his arms and began a lazy walk into the ocean.

"What are you doing?" She shrieked and wrapped her hands firmly around his neck.

"Cooling us off." He paused as the water reached his knees and when the next surge swept toward the shore, he treated them to a thorough dunk in the ocean water.

The rush of cold water should have shocked his system, but with Mallory in his arms and heat arcing between them, all it did was get him wet.

She was laughing as he carried her back to the large towel he'd set out on the sand. He placed her onto her feet and handed her a smaller hotel towel to dry off before settling himself besides her.

"Did it help?" she asked, as she ran the white terry over her hair and arms.

His body still throbbed with unslaked need and watching her movements beneath the sleek, wet suit, renewed desire hit him all over again.

He settled himself on the towel. "Didn't help a bit."

"I didn't think so." Without warning, she walked over, swung her leg around his waist and climbed into his lap.

He let out a groan. "Are you trying to kill me?"

"I'm just trying another alternative to solving your problem." She shifted until his hard flesh met her moist heat, the swimsuit barriers practically nonexistent. "I've heard the French call it a 'little death.'" A seductive gleam twinkled in her blue eyes.

He titled his head back, and staring at the night sky with its array of stars he grasped for control. "I *would* have to pick an educated smart-aleck woman."

She laughed lightly and snuggled more intimately astride him. "It's part of my charm."

He could think of many other attributes she possessed although right now he found it hard to think about anything else besides her body.

"And for the record, counselor, I believe I picked you first."

"I didn't know we were keeping track," he murmured, nuzzling her neck and letting his damp lips trail a blazing path on her soft skin.

She let out a soft exhale. "Liar. You were too keeping track or we wouldn't be here right now." Her back arched.

He caressed her neck and chest with laps of his tongue, tasting salt water and soft skin. It took some maneuvering, but he managed to ease her onto the towel, so she lay on her back and *he* sat on top, finally gaining control of the situation. Or so he thought until she parted her legs and allowed her thighs to cradle his erection in a cocoon of damp heat.

Complete access but no penetration, Jack thought and knew he was lost. His hips jerked forward. Mallory moaned aloud, but suddenly the sound of voices and laughter intruded on his passion-fogged brain.

He forced himself to focus. ''We're not alone anymore.''

Her long lashes fluttered against her pale skin. ''That's probably for the best.''

She was right but he disliked hearing it, especially coming from her well-kissed lips. *He* was the one usually pulling back from a woman and he damned well didn't enjoy being on the receiving end. Especially when the woman was Mallory.

Even in the darkness of the night, with the beach lit only by background hotel lighting, he could see where his razor stubble had chafed her flesh.

He swung his leg around and rolled off her. She raised a hand, covering her forehead and eyes from view, but she said nothing more. Her breathing was as labored and rough as his.

Long after the laughter had faded down the long stretch of beach, he lay by her side in silence. Surprisingly comfortable silence for two people still strung tight with arousal, caught in an awkward and potentially compromising situation.

He extended his arm and reached for her hand and she enclosed her fingers around his. Against the backdrop of the ocean roar, Jack realized he had accomplished his goal. He'd issued an invitation of his own and proved she was just as attracted, equally as affected by him as he was by her.

Alone, with no rules or interruptions, they couldn't keep their hands off each other.

They'd even begun to exchange memories—something completely foreign to him, yet utterly enjoyable.

But the score was even now. He had no excuse to challenge her again and the disappointment was strong, lingering and beyond anything he understood.

8

JACK WAS STILL WIRED after he said good-night to Mallory. His cold shower had done even less for his disposition than his state of arousal and sleep was impossible. He couldn't think of a damn thing except Mallory tossing and turning in the bed across the hall from his. Just because they had both agreed to part company before things went any further he didn't have to like it. He tossed off the covers and climbed out of bed.

Edgy and frustrated, he figured he might as well put his restless energy to use and get some work done. Hanging out at the bar and making small talk with the bartender might give him some insight into Paul Lederman. The elusive client. He pulled on a pair of jeans and an old University of Michigan sweatshirt, then took the elevator downstairs.

Jack glanced at his watch and was surprised at how late it actually was. At a summer resort the bar would normally be hopping, but last call had been half an hour ago and the place had emptied out. As he made his way inside the room, he realized he hadn't been the only one who couldn't sleep. His associate had the same idea of hanging out with the bartender, only

Mallory had cozied up to him in a way Jack never could.

Apparently playing the helpless woman at the pool table had gotten her close to the surly guy. Close in a way Jack didn't like at all. He clenched his hands into fists as he watched Mallory, dressed in form-fitting jeans, lean over the pool table so the bartender, a blond-haired surfer type, could press up behind her and correct her form.

She tossed her hair back and laughed at something the bartender whispered in her ear. Jack's gut clenched with jealousy. A foreign emotion for him when it came to women. A shocking one when it came to Mallory. He'd been with attractive women before, eager women, women he'd actually had sex with, but he'd always been able to cut them loose with no regrets or second thoughts.

So why with this woman? The one he worked with, who could jeopardize his career with one whisper. Perhaps it was the forbidden that attracted him, since their rendezvous could only be conducted in secret. Maybe it was the excitement of the chase, the challenge she posed that intrigued him so. As his body, still strung tight, reminded him, it could also be the lack of closure to the relationship that tugged at his gut.

He couldn't put her behind him. Not yet, anyway. It was time he stepped up the challenge.

He strode forward into the light surrounding the pool table. "Mind if I join the game?"

At the sound of his voice, Mallory groaned while

the bartender turned his head to acknowledge the intrusion. "Bar's closed," he said.

Jack leaned an elbow on the wooden edge of the table and nodded at Mallory. "She looks like a customer to me."

Mallory narrowed her gaze and shot him a scathing glance.

"She's a guest of the house. You can come back tomorrow night. Drinks on the house." The bartender turned his concentration back to Mallory, or rather, to her waist. He gripped his hands around the bare skin of her midriff, where her shirt had drifted upward.

Anger Jack hadn't experienced in ages rushed to the surface along with another memory—of coming home early from school at age fifteen to find a stranger and his mother exiting the bedroom she shared with Jack's father, the stranger's hands on his mother's waist as he helped her snap her pants closed.

But unlike his mother, Mallory didn't giggle and lean closer. She stiffened and would have moved away but for the pool table in front of her and the bartender's strong arms holding her in place. Whatever her earlier act, she was obviously through with the man now.

"Doesn't look like she wants to be that kind of a guest." Jack spoke through clenched teeth.

Sparks flashed in Mallory's blue eyes, emotion and anger aimed at him. "*She* can speak for herself."

She turned her gaze to the bartender and fluttered her lashes in a gesture Jack had never witnessed from Mallory before. "Looks like my friend doesn't know when a lady's playing hard to get, Jimmy," she said in a lazy drawl. But she casually moved his hand away from her waist.

"You know this guy?" The bartender jerked a finger Jack's way. From the sneer on the man's face, Jack figured any hope he'd had of gleaning information about Lederman was long gone.

"We work together." Mallory let out a long-suffering sigh and took a step back from Jimmy, tripping over his sneakered feet and nearly toppling to the floor in the process. Jack tried to reach for her at the same time as the bartender but she lunged onto the pool table and steadied herself first.

"Oops." She let out an un-Mallory-like laugh. "Those darn Long Island Iced Teas." She batted her eyelashes again and glanced at Jack. "Did you know they have a drink named after this area? Well sort of this area. Long Island Iced Tea. He makes them extra special," she said, smiling at the bartender. "Think I can have the recipe?"

"I think you've had enough." Jack had no doubt she wasn't drunk, just trying to keep the bartender off balance and intrigued. He stepped forward and grabbed her elbow before his competition could get to Mallory first.

"Don't you think the lady can decide when she has or hasn't had enough?" the bartender spoke.

Mallory bestowed her sweetest smile upon him. "A man who respects a lady's mind. I like that."

"Did you forget our early morning meeting?" Jack asked pointedly. "With Mr. Lederman?" He tossed Jimmy's employer's name into the mix and got the reaction he'd hoped for.

Jimmy stiffened. "You work with Lederman?"

Mallory clenched her jaw, clearly unhappy with Jack invading her territory. "He's considering using my firm. I thought I mentioned that."

"Before or after you pumped me for information?"

Mallory shrugged and smiled sweetly. "I'm a people watcher by nature. You wouldn't hold that against me, would you? Tell you what, why don't we meet up again when *he's* not around?" She elbowed Jack in the side.

Jack stifled a grunt but before he could speak, the bartender shook his head. "The boss'll have my head for consorting with the guests," he muttered. "Not that he wouldn't appreciate your charms himself but I need this job."

"Smart move," Jack said, making note of his reference to Lederman's taste for the ladies.

Jimmy scowled. "She's all yours, buddy."

"I'm not anyone's," Mallory muttered. "Especially his."

Jack grinned. "She doesn't know what she's saying, do you sweetheart?"

The bartender cursed beneath his breath and headed back to the bar to clean up for the night. Obviously he didn't like the idea of Jack getting the better of him, but when he put his testosterone aside, he knew his job came first.

Jack turned to his colleague. "Time to get you upstairs." Without waiting for a reply he lifted her into his arms and over one shoulder. "See ya around," he called out to the bartender who was still cursing and nursing his wounded pride.

Jimmy glanced over and caught sight of Jack's caveman routine and Mallory's flailing fists. He laughed hard. "Maybe you're not so bad. You come by tomorrow," he said to Jack. "Drinks are still on the house."

Mallory punched helplessly at Jack's back until the last shot hit a kidney.

Jack grunted. "You got it," he called. "Maybe we can compare notes."

"Put me down," Mallory yelled at him.

The bartender laughed again. Jack left the bar and made a quick right to the bank of elevators. He had no desire to cause a scene in the lobby.

Once inside the private elevator, he deposited Mallory on her feet.

"Just in time." She pulled down on her shirt and glared at him.

"I know." Right before he'd freed her, he'd felt her soft hands inching inside the waistband of his jeans searching for the elastic on his underwear.

He burst out laughing. "An older brother teach you that dirty trick?"

She shook her head. "I'm an only child. And you were this close to singing soprano." She held her thumb and forefinger together.

"I'd have to be wearing underwear for that weapon to work."

Her eyebrows arched in surprise and her blue eyes darkened with the possibility he was telling the truth.

He leaned back against the chrome and mirrored wall.

A grin formed on her lips as she stepped closer. "Prove it."

"What?"

Her fingers reached for the snap on his jeans as his breath caught in anticipation and desire. "You said no underwear. I want you to prove it."

His groin, free from constraints except for the hard denim wanted to do just that, but he held on to her wrists and met her gaze.

Her face was inches from his, her warm breath with barely a hint of alcohol rushed over his skin.

"How'd you keep surfer boy's hands off you?" he asked.

She tilted her head to the side. "Are you jealous? I admit he has a great body and a gorgeous tan, but…"

That did it. Jack silenced her with a kiss. It started slow but quickly blazed out of control. His tongue, her tongue, his groan, her heartfelt sigh—he couldn't tell the difference as they melded together. Like a dying man at an oasis, he drank from her, taking all she offered, all she had to give. And he gave back in kind, until they parted, coming up for air.

Her dazed blue eyes opened wide. "You *were* jealous."

He sucked in a deep breath of air. "Not a chance, sweetheart." But his thudding heart called him a liar. He stepped back and contemplated her. "So how'd you keep the bartender talking and not groping?" He grasped for mundane conversation, anything to give him time to regain his equilibrium.

"I sat next to a huge potted plant in the corner,

ordered drinks, nursed them while I inflated his ego, dumped them when he served other customers.''

He grinned. ''You are something.''

She averted her eyes. ''Why haven't the doors opened yet?''

He glanced around for the first time and realized neither of them had pushed the button for their floor.

He punched in the button for the fifth floor. The mechanism kicked into gear and they began their ascent. ''Elementary.''

''Then how come neither one of us thought of it?''

He reached out and fingered a strand of her hair. ''Because we were distracted?''

''By your caveman routine. Which reminds me, don't you ever carry me anywhere again.''

''Or what?'' The doors opened and he escorted her out of the elevator, his hand on her back.

She paused to turn and meet his gaze. ''I'll have to teach you a lesson, of course.'' Laughter danced in her eyes.

''Of course you would.'' And he'd get himself another invitation. He hoped. ''Give me your key. I'll help you get the door.''

Her expression turned wary.

''Friends help friends, okay?'' She reached into her pocket.

''Let's meet up for breakfast and discuss what you learned about Lederman. He left a message saying he'll be back the day after tomorrow and I'd like to be prepared.'' Although Jack was frustrated by the continued delay, part of him was grateful for the extra time alone with Mallory that Lederman's absence provided.

"Can we make it lunch? I'm beat." She pressed her card key into his palm.

"Sure thing." Then, knowing exactly how she'd respond, he picked her up once more and tossing her over his shoulder, headed for her door.

She didn't fight him. Instead she ran her fingers through his hair. "You'll pay for that," she murmured.

"That's what I was hoping for."

THANKS TO MALLORY, Jack awoke early, something that was becoming a habit on this pseudo-vacation. After carrying her into her room and depositing her on the bed, he'd stayed for one lingering good-night kiss before making himself scarce.

But part of him wished they'd never met up at the hotel bar last night. Both the jealousy and caveman routine were foreign to him. He hadn't recognized the blatant anger or possessive feelings Mallory aroused in him. Even as he'd realized her intent was to gain information from the bartender, the primal urge to carry her out and make an ass of himself had taken over.

After a long morning workout and soothing shower, Jack headed for the restaurant to meet Mallory. He took what had become his usual seat in the café, ordered black coffee, and rubbed a hand over his face, wondering when sanity would return.

When he caught sight of her talking with the hostess, he realized the answer was a resounding *never*.

Jack was destined to live in this perplexing, arousing hell created by one Mallory Sinclair.

This morning she'd exchanged her navy dress for a gray one, and the bun for a clip that held her hair away from her face in an equally severe style.

He shook his head. Jack saw Mallory's beauty inside and out, and his desire was no longer diminished by her deliberately harsh daytime appearance, yet his level of frustration with her duality grew.

Few male heads turned as she made her way to his table, and though Jack took pleasure in the fact that only *he* knew Mallory the seductress, a perverse part of him wanted other men to envy him for having this incredible woman by his side. He found himself wishing she'd show herself for the sensual woman she really was.

He was determined to find out the reasons behind the change.

True she wanted to make partner in their male dominated firm and saw downplaying herself as the means. And considering the old guard distrusted women and only grudgingly gave Mallory their respect, Jack understood. But he didn't have to like it. She deserved to be acknowledged for her abilities and accepted as the woman he knew her to be—nothing hidden, nothing feigned.

Although why he cared so much about how she chose to handle herself, her appearance and career remained a mystery to him. So did the reasons she kept up the charade here and now.

"Hi." As she slid into the chair across from him,

the desire to free her hair and watch it spill over her shoulders grew stronger.

"Hi, yourself."

She set her bag down by her side. "I'd kill for a cup of coffee."

He slid his freshly poured, untouched cup across the table. "Go ahead, it's on me."

She treated him to a grateful smile, one that transformed her face with an ethereal glow and put light into her eyes. He wondered if he was the only one who could see beyond the heavy black frames to the sparkling blue gaze beneath.

"No contacts today?" he asked.

"Nope." She shook the napkin out and placed it in her lap.

"Because it's daytime."

"Correct. What are you having for breakfast?"

"An omelette." He didn't want her to change the subject before he could dig deeper. "Would you wear contacts if you were on vacation?"

She shrugged. "I'm not on vacation, I'm working."

"No one here is from the office." He gestured around the tourist-filled room.

"Except you." She gave him a penetrating glare.

Both the look and the point grated. "So you trust my silence for whatever happens between us at night, but you don't trust me during the day?"

Mallory let out a long-suffering sigh. "You miss the point. No one else from the office is here but Lederman is due back soon and he's unpredictable enough to show up unexpectedly. He works with the higher-ups and would probably love to talk. Then there's Mrs. Lederman. Though she's accommodating now, she can turn any time when she realizes it's in her best interest."

"And last night's show?"

She dropped her shoulders in resignation. "I wanted information but I won't risk going out in public like that again."

Jack hated to admit she had valid points, only because it meant suffering through the torment of waiting till evening to see *his* Mallory again. With the ball in her court, he had no idea if or when he would see her again.

Frustration filled him. "Omelette for you, too?" he asked, changing the subject.

"Pancakes with a side order of bacon. A glass of orange juice. Oh, and coffee, please."

The waitress, who had made her way over, jotted down their orders, then took the menus back from Mallory.

"Worked up an appetite last night, did you?" he asked.

Mallory pursed her lips, obviously wanting to smack him in his inflated ego. Jack grinned, enjoying teasing her and knowing she wouldn't stay mad long. He waited for her carefully worded barb.

"Being carried off by a macho male has that effect on me," came out of her mouth instead. A blush crept onto her cheeks at the unexpected omission. "And the coffee's for you."

He let out a loud laugh and the people at the neighboring table turned to look. She narrowed her eyes and glared, but instead of sobering, the more frustrated she got, the harder he chuckled.

"Can I help it if that scene you made brought out the worst in me?" Jack stopped laughing. His feelings last night were no joke.

"I had no idea you'd show up."

"But once I did, you enjoyed it." His stare never wavered.

"Maybe for a minute." She bit down on her lower lip and leaned closer. Her honest blue eyes bore into his. "And only because I thought that jealousy bit was an act," she said.

Surprise at her admission caught him off guard. His self-confident colleague had turned into a vulnerable woman. He'd never have believed it if he hadn't heard her say so out loud.

He leaned closer, too, until their lips were inches apart and their breaths mingled. "That was no act."

"At some point I realized that. But I never thought you'd react that way about me."

"I sure as hell didn't expect it either. Not at first glance."

She tipped her head to the side, a serious expression crossing her face. "I appreciate the honesty."

"Good. But I'm not finished yet." Unable to get closer as she physically withdrew across the table, he grabbed for her hand instead. "I wasn't jealous only because I've seen the seductress in you. I was jealous because I'm intrigued by you. By *all* of you."

Her mouth opened and closed but no sound came out.

"Care to tell me why you wouldn't think I'd be interested enough to get jealous?"

Considering the physical sensations that arced between them, Jack couldn't understand why she'd doubted the sincerity and strength of that emotion.

She shrugged, then said simply, "Because no one's ever reacted possessively with me."

"Then I'd have to say you've had a string of stupid men in your life."

She grinned. "And I'd have to agree with you."

He tightened his grip around her smaller hand. "This inability to see yourself as you should—that comes from where?" Because no woman deliberately dressed herself down and downplayed such incredible looks without a damn good reason.

Her lips shut as if she could stop the truth from coming out by sheer willpower alone.

"Bad relationship?" he hazarded a guess.

"Bad upbringing," she shot back, then opened her eyes wide at the realization that things were finally out in the open between them.

"Go on." He sat back and waited, but didn't release her hand, knowing their emotional connection could only be strengthened by physical touch.

"First I was an accident, then I was a disappointment. My father wanted a boy. He got me instead." As she spoke, the light in her expressive eyes dimmed. "Over time I learned not to expect too much."

"And your parents never delivered."

"Right."

He shook his head, anger and frustration filling him

at two people who'd created a child and then proceeded to negate her sense of self-worth. He'd at least had his father behind him. Mallory had had herself—and she'd managed to chart her own destiny.

In Jack's mind, she'd taken the wrong course. Hiding herself couldn't make her happy for long, but only she could realize that truth. If he happened to nudge her in the right, sensual direction, he'd be happy to help her out. Not just for selfish reasons but because she deserved to experience all life had to offer—and not see those wonderful things skewed behind thick, oblique lenses.

"Your parents were wrong, you know."

She shrugged, but her intense stare told him she was listening.

He wondered if she believed him and made it his mission to be sure she was paying attention. "And it's their loss—missing out on *you*."

Her eyes filled with moisture, gratitude evident. She inhaled a shaky breath. "Thanks again. Truth's a wonderful thing and I don't hear it much."

An emotional lump formed in his throat. "When I'm with you, my body tells you exactly how I'm feeling. What's the point in lying now?" As if by suggestion, he shifted in his seat to alleviate the sudden discomfort in his groin.

"Anyone ever tell you you're a nice guy?" Her lips lifted upward in a grin that warmed him and chased away the chill that had always surrounded his heart.

He shook his head. "I've never given anyone reason before."

Mallory struggled to calm her pounding heart. This connection between them was growing stronger. She felt it.

She wanted to run from it but didn't dare. Talking past her emotions wasn't easy but she owed Jack for easing a huge burden she'd always carried with her. "About the jealousy bit?" She changed the subject back to last night. "I didn't enjoy the act."

In fact, the bartender's sweaty palms and let-me-show-you-a-good-time attitude had turned her off from the beginning. Only her search for information had kept her rooted in her seat and had forced her to allow his unwanted attention.

"I didn't want him touching me." She gazed at Jack through heavy eyelids. "I wished it was you."

His skin drew tight over his cheekbones as awareness raced between them. "I appreciate you returning the favor," he said finally.

She knew he was referring to her honest answer and nodded. She'd give him even more honesty later. Because this conversation had proven to her without a doubt—she wasn't finished with Jack Latham.

"Now, care to tell me what you uncovered about Lederman?" Jack lowered his voice.

Grateful for normal conversation, Mallory looked around. The restaurant had grown more crowded and a low hum of voices droned on around them. They could easily talk in hushed tones without being overheard, or so she thought until she turned toward the hostess station.

Mallory let out a groan. "I wish I could, but Alicia

Lederman's doing the rounds of the tables, talking to customers.''

"Food's up." The waitress arrived with their plates, giving them yet another reason to postpone talking business.

He let out an equally frustrated sound. "Guess we've got to wait."

Mallory nodded and reached for her fork. Since this trip, she'd gotten good at waiting.

And even better at anticipation.

She finished her meal in record time, hunger for food satisfying one craving, while her need for Jack only grew.

JACK HAD PROMISED to wake Mallory from a late-afternoon nap but calls to his secretary and another client took longer than he'd expected. By the time he left the conference room Lederman had given him for business use and made his way back to their floor, Jack realized she was probably out sightseeing or walking on the beach. But he figured he'd give waking her a shot anyway, just in case.

"Wake up, Sleeping Beauty. Rise and shine." He knocked on her door.

"You looking for the Missus in the room?"

Jack turned.

A chambermaid stood behind him, an armload of towels in hand. "I saw her leave a little while ago."

His disappointment was keen. For no good reason, he knew, because he had no concrete plans—just a burning desire to see her again. And he couldn't control the disappointment building inside him because after their bonding session she'd thought nothing of disappearing without leaving him a message.

"Are you sure it was her? Dark hair, blue eyes."

"I'm sure. She asked me for fresh towels and..." The dark haired woman shook her head. "Never mind. Other folks' strange requests aren't my business."

He didn't question her further. "Well I appreciate the information."

She smiled. "No problem. You have a nice day." She let herself into Mallory's room carrying the towels and Jack began a retreat back into his own.

"Wait."

He turned back.

"I didn't realize you were the gentleman across the hall. She..." The woman pointed to Mallory's door. "She left something for you. I was going to leave it on your bed when I finished inside. Wait here."

She strode to her utility cart and returned with a white sheet of paper in one hand, an innocuous brown bag in the other. "These are for you."

"Thanks." His pulse picked up rhythm as he lifted the paper and inhaled the fragrant scent. Arousal hit him harder and stronger than ever before. So did the sense of anticipation.

One part of him knew she was answering his challenge from last night. Another part of him sensed she was responding to their new-found closeness today. He'd never experienced such intense feelings for another person—never wanted to make someone else feel better and ease their pain—until Mallory.

The thought scared him spitless so he focused on

the invitation instead. Waiting until he was alone in his room, he peered into the bag and pulled out the bottom half of a string bikini, too skimpy to cover anything at all.

His mouth went dry and he opened the sheet of paper and read aloud. "Our cabin at eight. Come for a romp on *my* beach." He fingered the nylon strings in his hands. He could come right now, he thought wryly.

A vision came to him, of Mallory wearing the matching top, nothing below. Jack broke into a sweat. He shook his head. No way would she have the nerve. Then he remembered she'd already gone skinny-dipping. She had also revealed her deepest emotions. Her nerve was greater than he'd realized.

The next couple of hours loomed long in front of him, but no doubt that was her intent. To leave him with the flimsy bottoms and lots of time on his hands to think.

And fantasize.

By the time eight o'clock rolled around, Jack was in a heated state of need. And by the time he arrived at the cottage door, his hands were shaking.

The woman knew how to drive him mad with suggestion and innuendo. If he believed in relationships, he'd think he'd found a woman who could engage and entice him, keep him interested for a lot longer than one night.

Good thing he didn't believe or he'd be in deep trouble. Jack raised his fist and knocked on the door.

9

MALLORY ANSWERED the door quickly, greeting him with an easy smile. "Hi, there."

"Hi, yourself." She'd left him hanging this afternoon with a skimpy piece of her bathing suit and a provocative invitation for tonight.

It hadn't been enough. He'd been a man deprived and he drank in the sight of her now.

She'd prepared for the beach.

He'd like to think she'd prepared for him.

Her top, if he could call it that, was the match for the bikini bottoms in his pocket. Two triangles, aqua in color and rimmed with white piping didn't quite cover her breasts and exposed more than a hint of soft flesh and cleavage. Whatever he'd envisioned, reality was sweeter. His mouth watered at the luscious view and his gaze traveled downward.

A matching scarf knotted at one hip, tied around her waist and ended midthigh. He had no clue what she wore beneath the blue sarong and the thought of her wearing no panties, no bottoms, nothing at all, made him crazy with curiosity and insane with longing. No doubt that had been her intent. As if she could read his thoughts, a provocative smile lifted the corner of her mouth.

She was making him pay for his caveman routine and he loved every minute.

She leaned against the doorframe, one arm propped against the wooden molding, her head tipped so that black curls fell over one shoulder. "You're prompt. I like that in a man."

Deliberately seductive and playful at the same time, she made him want to pull her into his arms and kiss her until neither one of them could think or breathe. "What else do you like?"

"Come on in and find out." She turned and sashayed inside, leaving him to follow. At this moment he'd go anywhere she led him and wasn't ashamed to admit it.

His gaze surveyed her barefooted retreat and the sultry sway of her hips beneath the blue skirt. She passed through the living room area they'd dined in before and continued into a short hallway. He wondered at her final destination and decided he enjoyed this kind of mystery and suspense.

"We're here." She paused at the entrance to the last door at the end.

He stopped inches away. Her skin glowed from time in the sun, and a light flush on her cheeks told him she was just as affected by this scenario as he was.

"You need to take off your shoes," she said.

He met her amused stare. "Because...?"

"Because we're going to the beach and you don't want to get sand in your shoes. Come on, Jack." She drawled out his name in a husky purr. "Use your imagination."

He reached out and fingered the hem on her make-shift skirt. "Trust me, sweetheart, my imagination's working just fine."

So were other strategic body parts. Wondering what the hell she had on beneath the short skirt would keep him erect all evening. He wondered how far she'd take this invitation and knew he couldn't wait to find out.

Her flush turned into a full-fledged blush. The blush intrigued him most of all. Although she toyed with him deliberately, he knew now the seductive charm and come-hither games didn't come easily to her. He sensed, too, that she didn't play like this often. Instead of sending him running, the possibility drew him deeper.

Jack had never been into too-innocent women, if only because they tended to expect too much in the end. But Mallory was different. She was provocative in a sultry, sexy way that turned him on and made him want to explore those uncharted waters. But she was also an independent, gutsy woman who wouldn't demand all from a man and give nothing in return.

She understood business, and he sensed she understood him, too. His heart pounded harder in his chest.

He slipped off his sneakers. "Lead the way."

She pushed open the door and he stepped inside. The scent of coconut hit him first, a warm fragrant aroma that reminded him of summers at the beach. He noticed the temperature next, a concentrated rise in heat from neon lights set up in the corner. Blow-up palm trees nestled around all four corners of the bed. And the sliding glass door leading to the beach had been opened, allowing a soft, humid breeze to drift inside.

"You like?" The hesitancy in her voice was clear. She'd obviously gone to a lot of thought and effort to set up this fantasy. Jack knew this had ceased being about teaching him a lesson and had become more about giving pleasure.

No woman other than Mallory had ever gone out of her way to do something for him. That she cared enough, was interested enough to bring illusion to life would tie him up in knots if he let it.

He'd rather just enjoy.

He reached out and grabbed for her hand. "I like."

Her soft fingers wrapped around his. "That's a good start. We could have sat outside but I thought we'd want a little more privacy, so I created our own beach." Husky undertones infused her voice with warmth and desire. "I figured we could hang out in here." She paused deliberately. "At least until dark."

She pulled him toward the bed and when she settled herself on the mattress and curled both knees to one side, Jack nearly died wondering if she'd reveal anything he so longed to see.

She followed the direction of his gaze and laughed. "You're naughty, you know that? Did you bring my bottoms?"

"Right here." He patted the front pocket of his swimsuit, which had grown increasingly tight.

Her gaze widened as she took in the obvious bulge in his shorts. The soft skin on her neck rose and fell as she swallowed hard. "If you behave maybe I'll let you see them on me."

A wicked gleam flickered in Jack's heated stare. "I'd rather see them off."

"What makes you think you aren't? Seeing them off me I mean?" She stood and made a provocative show of wiggling her behind. Used to frilly panties, the sensation of bare skin against cooler material felt wickedly decadent and erotic. She settled herself back on the bed.

He eased himself beside her. "You aren't daring me to check, are you?" His fingers inched towards her.

"And ruin the element of mystery and surprise? Not a chance." She playfully slapped his hand. "But you can get us ready for our swim." She grabbed the bottle of massage oil from the nightstand and handed it to him. "Do my back."

"It's nighttime."

She grinned. "And I thought we were using our imaginations. I wouldn't mind a little help getting the hard to reach spots." She stretched her legs out in front of her and wiggled her toes.

His eyes darkened as he accepted the bottle. "Do I get to call the spots?"

His hands on his choice of her body parts. A tremor of awareness shot through her veins. "If you think you can handle it."

He reached down and pulled at the hem of his T-shirt, lifting it up and over his head. "I assure you I can." His eyes bore into hers. "The question is can you?"

She stared at his broad chest, darkened from the summer sun and roughened with a sprinkling of dark hair. The man gave new meaning to the word sexy, she thought.

She managed a grin. "You know better than to throw a challenge my way." She pulled her hair to one side and stretched out further onto the bed. "Where do you want to start?"

She met his gaze, saw his eyes darkening. Then he opened the top of the bottle and poured a liberal amount of scented oil onto his palm.

"I'd like to start at the bottom and work my way up. But I also believe in saving the best for last, so roll onto your stomach and we'll begin with your back."

"Mmm. I can get into that." She sighed and rolled over, resting her chin on her hands. A back rub might help relax some of her tension and nerves and eliminate lingering insecurities that remained.

And then he straddled her back. Insecurities and most other thoughts fled. Though his weight was braced on his knees, the pressure of his firm backside and groin against her hips wouldn't be denied. An erotic tingling suffused her body and a throbbing beat of anticipation took hold.

Relax? She should have known better. This was foreplay. A distinct tremor rippled through her.

"You doing okay?" he asked.

"Great."

"Then let's begin." His voice came out a low rumble and then warm, hot hands touched her back, branding her skin.

He began a slow lubrication of her shoulders, smoothing his palms over her upper back and down her arms with practiced ease. Gentle pressure alternated with harder thrusts, giving her the massage she'd desired while covering her body with oil. The distinctive scent of coconut assaulted her, wrapping her in a heated cocoon of warmth and desire.

She searched her mind for conversation, something to break the awareness and allow her some control. "This feels wonderful," she said instead.

So much for control. But she admitted, she didn't want anything mundane to interrupt the heady sensations he was stirring inside her.

"That's the point." His deep laugh reverberated against her. He didn't stop his gentle ministrations as he spoke. "Listen to the crashing waves. I rent a beach house for two weeks at the end of every summer. You can't beat the relaxation or solitude."

She had to agree. The ebb and flow of the tide sounded much like the rushing of blood in her veins, soothing yet arousing at the same time. "A beach house of your own and you haven't made time for skinny-dipping?"

"No more than you've made time for vacations I bet."

"Unfortunately I can't afford the time off." His fingers rounded her shoulders and moved up her neck. He hit the spots that held the most tension and as her muscles relaxed, her awareness rose.

"You could if you wanted to." He leaned forward. All heat and hard male body, he trapped her between him and the mattress. "You could if you put yourself first. Before that all-consuming need to impress people whose love should be given unconditionally."

His implication was clear. Her drive for partnership was for the wrong reasons.

"Besides you know what they say about all work and no play," he said before she could respond. His voice sounded close and his breath fanned her ear. Her nipples hardened in response, pressing against the bed.

She swallowed a moan. "All work and no play," she murmured. "It makes Mallory a partner one day." But right now the dream that had sustained her most of her life seemed distant and far away. Unimportant in comparison to the sensual feelings rioting through her.

Unimportant compared to being with Jack.

She'd begun to suspect he had valid points about her reasons for pushing so hard for partnership and losing her sense of self. But no way she'd waste a minute of her precious time with him dissecting her possible mistakes. She had the rest of her life to do that. She'd rather enjoy now.

He sat up and suddenly she felt a tugging on the back tie of her bathing suit.

"Jack..." Warning laced her voice.

"Relax."

"He says as he pulls off my top."

He laughed. "I just untied it." His fingertip traced the line where her bathing suit had been and she arched her back in response.

God, the man was good. If he could arouse her with simple words and innocent touches against her skin, heaven help her when the real sexual play began.

"But I haven't pulled it off. Yet." His warm palms

pressed hard against her back. His hands wrapped around her ribs and sides, his fingertips inching toward her swollen breasts that ached for his firm touch.

She let out a small whimper, and when he eased her from her stomach onto her back, she rolled willingly and gazed into his eyes. The top string of her bathing suit remained tied, but the material slipped revealing her to his gaze.

His expression, darkened with need and desire, met her stare. She swallowed hard as she wondered what erogenous zone he'd touch next. So far every part of her body had turned into a mass of writhing need beneath his hands.

Without breaking eye contact, he pulled her to a sitting position, reached for the bikini top and drew it over her head. She fought the urge to cover herself and was rewarded by the clench of his jaw and a low, guttural groan.

The knowledge that he obviously liked what he saw eased her embarrassment enough to let her get playful again. "I thought we were getting ready for the sun," she said, reminding him to use his imagination.

"And I hoped you could teach me the fine art of skinny-dipping. Seeing as how you're a pro and all." One side of his mouth lifted in a charming grin she'd bet had devastated more women than she could count on both hands.

Her heart leapt to her throat. "It's something to consider. Later."

"Okay then in the meantime, I don't want to miss any sensitive areas."

He poured some more oil into his palms and rubbed

them together. "I'm warming them," he explained, in answer to her questioning look.

Mallory couldn't draw her stare from the sight of his large hands or her thoughts from the hope that he would use them to cover her breasts and satisfy the desire aching inside her.

"Come here." He crooked his finger at her.

Mesmerized by the husky gravel in his voice and the lure of his touch, she moved forward on the bed and settled in front of him, seated on her knees.

He mimicked her position. Thanks to his greater height, he seemed to tower over her. Anticipation rose within her but Jack did nothing to rush his movements or put an end to her expectation.

Then slowly, his eyes never leaving hers, he leaned forward and captured her lips in a kiss. His mouth was warm and hot, giving but intense. He devoured her with nibbles and slow licks of his tongue. And just when she thought she was lost in him, those hot hands cupped her waiting breasts.

The unexpected touch sent a jolt of sensation to her core and she moaned. She would normally have been mortified, but his reaction obliterated all rational thought. He deepened the kiss, making love to her with his mouth while his hands began an exploration all their own. He squeezed gently with the edge of his fingers while pressing insistently against her nipples with his splayed palm. She grabbed hold of his hips to anchor herself against the dizzying, spiraling waves of need.

She couldn't say who broke the kiss first. She was shaking with need and desire and shock. She'd never been so wanton or responded to a man with the intensity with which she responded to Jack. The knowledge gave her pause and she scooted back to the headboard, seeking space.

His eyes were glazed and unfocused, much like hers, she assumed since he looked as shaken as she felt. Silence pulsed between them.

Mallory leaned back against a bank of throw pillows. She glanced around for a covering for her exposed skin, but found nothing within reach. She settled for closing her eyes against the sight and feeling of being raw and exposed.

But all she saw beneath shut eyelids was Jack, rubbing his hands together and her imagination conjured the feel of his slickened palms against her still tingling, still wanting flesh.

"I haven't finished protecting you from the sun."

At the sound of his husky voice, she trembled. Shaken or not, when the man started a project, he apparently liked to finish. Something they had in common. Because she hadn't finished wanting him.

"Then what are you waiting for?" Funny how she found bravery beneath closed eyes.

His hot fingers grabbed hold of her foot and began a slow, easy massage. He kneaded and rubbed, pressed and released, eliciting a torturous yet rapturous sensation at the same time. He coated her foot and calf with scented oil, pausing to relubricate his hands before doing the same to the other leg and then moving upward.

He'd only grasped her ankle yet the rest of her flesh burned. He built up the steady press and release rhythm anew, one her body seemed to recognize and mimic until the pulsing of her muscles found an answering vibration in areas he had yet to caress.

"I have to admit, you've got talent," she said on a soft sigh, opening her eyes.

"You haven't seen anything yet." He met her gaze with a lingering look that felt more like a caress. His smile obviously meant to reassure.

His hands eased up from her knee to just above the hem of her skirt. When he touched skin, his eyes widened in surprise. "No bottoms."

"Of course not. They're in your pocket," she said, treating him to what she hoped was a disarming grin and a teasing glint in her eyes. Bravado was all she had left to rely on. He'd seen and felt everything else. "You doubted me."

"I doubted your nerve," he conceded. His fingers swept in broad strokes across her femininity and her breath caught in her throat. "But I shouldn't have." His features darkened. "And if you want me to stop, I will. Just say the word."

Jack's hands closed around her thighs. He leaned over her, his dark head bowed so she looked directly into his compelling and intense gaze.

His thumb grazed tingling flesh that had been deprived for too long. He initiated long, smooth strokes that tantalized and teased, seduced and captivated.

"Stop?" She'd die if he did.

The delicious movement of his fingertips paused. His dark eyes questioned. And Mallory feared she'd broken the spell and she'd never feel the culmination of his fervent ministrations.

She licked her lips, coating the dry skin. "That was a rhetorical question." In fact she was more afraid of him stopping than of him taking the next step.

Relief washed over his handsome features, but he didn't say a word, just reached for the bottle once more. He poured a quarter-sized amount of liquid into his hand. "The sun can be deadly to skin that's not used to the harsh rays."

"So I've heard." Her heart began to pound hard and fast, but somehow she managed a smile. One meant to reassure him she wanted everything and anything he planned.

His grin was nothing short of intoxicating as he parted the scarf she'd tied around her waist earlier and slipped his hands beneath the material. "In fact, I'd better make sure I coat every inch." His entire palm cupped her thigh so his fingertips merely grazed her private folds.

The tingling she'd felt earlier turned into a full-fledged blaze. A teasing hint of what was to come, and her hips jerked upward of their own volition. "I…" She realized the sound came out more a moan than a coherent word. "I'm burning now."

"But you're burning from me, not the sun." His slick fingers met her waiting flesh.

Dizzying sensations assaulted her as hot, coated strokes of his fingertips parted and caressed. She moaned as he kneaded her in exactly the right place. The moan turned her into a wild woman, her hips bucking against his hand.

Jack muttered a soft curse. Sweet heaven. And that's where he was, in heaven, with a woman more responsive, more open and giving than any he'd known. Dampness coated his hand and despite the slick oil, he knew he'd found her essence. His own body throbbed but he couldn't relieve his or her passion that way. No matter how much he wanted to.

No matter how much he wanted her.

Because this romp on the beach had taught him something about himself. He could lose himself in this woman. After all he'd seen in his jaded youth, life and career, there was no way he could allow it. But he could enjoy her warmth and heat and revel in giving *her* pleasure with no threat to himself.

He glanced down at her delicate features. Her eyes were shut tight, her face alight with passion. He was in control of her emotions and her release. And that's all that mattered.

Each movement and caress of his hand elicited a new response. Enthralled by the pure rapture and need he saw on her face, the temptation to prolong his exquisite torture was appealing. But not at her expense and though she was obviously enjoying it, he'd also brought her too close, too fast.

He did the only thing he could. He eased his finger inside her hot, moist body. She shook and convulsed around him, and then her body squeezed his finger tight, gripping him in damp heat and complete ecstasy.

He stretched out beside her. With his free hand, he smoothed long strands of hair off her face. ''Look at me.''

Her velvet blue eyes opened wide and she met his gaze with an imploring one of her own. He shifted his hand. Without withdrawing his finger, he cupped her entire mound in his palm and rotated with gentle pressure.

"Jack." Her eyelids opened wide as she breathed his name.

"I'm here." His thumb moved in small circles until her breathing came in shallow labored gasps.

He'd found the right spot, the one that made her wild. The one that made her his. Maintaining a steady rhythm and keeping a slickened finger inside her body, he edged her closer and closer to the precipice.

"Go with it, sweetheart." He urged her on with his words and his calculated movements until her climax hit fast and furious.

He *felt* the shudders wracking her body, relentless in intensity and just as he thought she was coming down off the crest, he pressed his palm one last time against the juncture of her thighs. She let out a sound that was a groan of utter pleasure and surrender.

Jesus, she was hot and wild and her uninhibited moan rocked the foundation of his world. He'd give almost anything to experience the same moment *inside* her body.

Almost. Because after the intense reactions they'd both experienced with just a kiss, if he made love to Mallory, Jack feared neither one of them would find their way back to a sane, solitary life.

Her spasms stopped as quickly as they'd come and he found himself gazing into her sated deep blue eyes. Minutes passed in silence. Finally, when her labored breathing reached a normal rate, she spoke.

"You give new meaning to protection from the sun."

He was glad she'd taken things lightly. After the intimate moments in this bedroom, he feared she'd get too serious.

Then he laughed wryly. Perhaps *he* was at risk of losing himself to this woman who'd begun to trust him with her most personal demons and secrets, but he couldn't say she felt the same. At least she hadn't been in control of herself seconds earlier, he thought smugly.

"Wipe that self-satisfied grin off your face before I'm forced to take drastic action." She pulled her skirt down and pushed herself to a sitting position, hugging her knees against her exposed breasts. All without meeting his gaze.

So she wasn't the woman of the world she wanted him to think she was. The thought gave Jack immense pleasure. Not that he had any delusions that he was her first anything, but he could tell from the shy way she cast her eyes from him and the becoming flush on her cheeks that Mallory wasn't overly experienced in dealing with things afterward. She was most definitely the enigma he'd painted her as, with more intriguing facets revealing themselves to him as time passed.

He reached for her bathing suit top and draped it over her head. Gratitude filled her gaze, warming him, caressing him in her essence. He swiveled her to the side and retied the open strings of the bikini at her back.

All without sound or roaming hands. No matter

how much he desired to leave her bared to his gaze, she'd obviously be more comfortable covered. And her comfort mattered more to him than a lingering glance at her bare breasts or an extra stroke with his hands. Being with Mallory was hot and electric, but it was more than a casual sexual encounter he'd leave behind in the morning and forget by the next day.

Jack wasn't stupid and knew there was an important subliminal message in his feelings regarding this affair, but he chose not to heed it. Affair being the operative term, a brief interlude where they could both indulge their sensual natures.

He shifted positions so he moved back in front of her again.

"Thank you." Emotion flickered in her gaze.

He flashed her a charming, light grin. "You're welcome." He cupped her chin in his hand and brushed his thumb over her silken skin. "The whole point was to give you pleasure."

She laughed. "You know I meant thank you for the bathing suit, not thank you for the..." A red-hot blush stained her cheeks and she shook her head. "Never mind that. But the whole point was to entice you."

"And you did it very well. In a very unique way."

She rolled her eyes. "I didn't mean that the way it sounded. Every woman in the office wants to entice you. I'm not a Terminator groupie. But you challenged me and I just wanted..." Her voice trailed off, and he got the distinct impression she figured, why bother explaining.

But he desired an explanation. Badly. He knew

women were drawn to him, but he never took the attention seriously. He figured they liked a challenge and a partner-challenge made him even more of a catch in their eyes. He tended to ignore both the gossip and the interest. But Mallory was different and he never wanted her to feel grouped with a bunch of women whose notice he neither encouraged nor wanted.

He bent closer. So close he could brush his lips over hers, and without thought, he did. She leaned into him, softening her mouth against his and he accepted her encouragement, drawing her into a moist kiss, more meaningful and less urgent than before. Then he pulled back. "You wanted to what?" he asked softly.

Her lashes fluttered upward. "To show you what it's like to be an optimist, like we discussed the other day on the beach. To give you something to dream about when our time together is over." Wide eyes stared up at him, drawing him in with her honesty and sweetness.

"You wanted me to dream about you."

She inclined her head in a slight nod. "The same way I've dreamed about you," she admitted.

He was flattered, but realized he didn't like the end of their relationship being discussed aloud. Especially coming from her luscious, well-kissed lips. Even if she was right and an end was inevitable.

He leaned back, his chin resting on his knees as he studied her flushed face. "I'll dream about you, Mallory. In ways I've never dreamed about anyone else."

She met and held his gaze. Warmth and bonding

bounced between them before she shook her head and broke the spell. She smiled. "Why don't you hand over the oil and let me give you more for the memory books?" Her lips turned upward into a wicked grin. "You're not the only one who can satisfy."

10

JACK'S BODY HARDENED at the thought of Mallory's soft hands on his straining erection. "And I know you were satisfied."

"Typical man." She laughed. "Come on. Let me have the oil. We can't have you taking that body in the sun without adequate coverage."

Coverage. He liked that thought. Jack passed the bottle toward her. "Careful it's slippery."

"Oh, I think I can handle it." Her fingers deliberately touched his before wrapping around the top of the bottle neck, in a provocative grip meant to show him she knew exactly how to handle a slippery appendage.

Then she crooked a finger his way.

He swallowed a groan. "You sure you want to continue this on the bed?"

She shrugged. "I'm not sleeping here, just fulfilling fantasies. Quit stalling, Jack." She leaned back against the pillows and spread her legs wide, patting the space in between.

Though her skirt covered everything, his imagination and those memories she mentioned were vivid. As he slid into the welcoming vee of her legs, he recalled her warm moist heat around his hand and her soft sighs of satisfaction.

"Relax." Her slick hands gripped his shoulders. "I'm just going to protect you from those harsh rays you talked about."

But who would protect him from her potent allure?

He shut his eyes and let her work. Her coating of his back and shoulders went fine. He enjoyed her gentle ministrations and had just begun to relax as she requested...when her fingers slipped around his abdomen and lingered, palms splayed against his ribs and her fingers inches from his nipples.

His breath caught in his throat.

"What happened to relaxing?" Her soft voice blew in his ear, strengthening his arousal.

"You're joking right? You want me to relax when a beautiful woman's got me wrapped in her arms?"

Her hands stilled and her arms tightened around his chest. "You think I'm beautiful?"

The hesitancy in her voice touched him in a place precariously close to his heart. "How could you not know?"

She laughed and he sensed if he turned, he'd see more emotion than he could handle. He already knew he was drawn to her, but if he saw the vulnerability in her eyes and the sensitivity in her gaze, he'd be in deeper waters than he could comfortably tread.

"For one thing, you admitted it in the restaurant when you said you wouldn't have expected to fall for me at first glance."

He cringed. "I didn't mean it that way."

"I didn't take it as an insult. You reacted to me

exactly how I want people to react. I'm Mallory, the office ice queen. I get up in the morning and pull my hair into a bun. I splash cold water on my face, put on some moisturizer and I head out the door. In conservative suits and sensible shoes.''

''And I now know why. What I don't know is why continue? You're a smart, intelligent woman. Why play the part when you don't need to prove yourself to anyone? And don't tell me because that's the real you, or start playing games about which Mallory is real, okay? Considering what we just did, you can answer that one question.''

He felt rather than saw her shift uneasily. ''I have my reasons.''

''Not good enough.''

She started to push away, to withdraw.

''Don't go.''

She paused, then relaxed behind him. He leaned back, letting skin touch skin. He wanted to feel her and he knew maintaining a physical connection was his only chance of getting an honest answer.

When she remained silent, he dove in with his best guess. ''Because after years of dressing the part, you don't know the real you either?''

He felt her slight nod. ''Maybe.''

Her hair fell forward, brushing his shoulders. The sensation, soft and feathery light, caused him to shake with renewed desire. But he sensed her need for reassurance and maybe something more.

''There's a part of me that loves what I do. Don't think my life has been such a sacrifice. I'm not ready to throw a pity party so don't you go getting maudlin on me either.''

He laughed. "There's many things I feel for you, sweetheart. Pity isn't one of them.''

She scooted forward until her breasts pushed insistently against his back.

"Play fair,'' he warned her. "Your parents set you on this course so what's your mother's role in all this?'' He reached back and squeezed her wrists, the only silent reassurance he could give.

"She loves my father. His disappointment was her disappointment. Do we have to talk about this when there's so many other things we could do instead?'' Her fingernails raked along his back in an overtly provocative move.

"You're talking to someone who's made *not* dealing with his parents an art form.'' After her revelation, he felt he owed her that much truth.

And besides, he understood only too well what it felt like to have a painful childhood affect the present. Of course in Jack's case at least he had one parent proud of his accomplishments. Hers underestimated a child they ought to be proud of, and created a woman who didn't know her own worth.

"You're beautiful.'' He could give her an honest infusion of truth in return for the fantasies she'd created for him.

She let out a sigh of disbelief. "I've looked in a mirror, Jack.''

Those contradictions again. And the old question—which was the real Mallory.

"Don't move.'' He swung his legs off the bed and

headed to the corner of the room where a large floor-length mirror with gilded wrought iron leaves stood. He pushed the mirror into the room and parked it at the foot of the bed.

She eyed the object warily. "What's that for?"

"Before we get on with the beach theme, I wanted to get some things between us perfectly clear."

After positioning the mirror, Jack moved behind her and gripping her shoulders, he turned her so she had no choice but to stare into the reflective glass.

"Take a look and memorize what you see. Because next time you doubt, I want you to glance into a mirror and see yourself through *my* eyes."

Mallory glanced into the large glass and winced. As if she had a choice whether or not to look with the darn thing in her face.

"Because *I* see a well-satisfied woman."

Mallory agreed. In her flushed face, she saw the aftereffects of her orgasm hadn't diminished. Her cheeks were shaded a light pink, her eyes still bright and alive with sensual awareness.

He walked back to the mirror and turned so he stood with one hand slung over the top of the wrought iron. "But I also see a beautiful woman, inside as well as out."

A grateful yet embarrassed grin lifted her lips. "You do have a way with words, counselor."

He shook his head. "Truth is truth. No one's ever gone so out of their way for me. You've done it. Twice."

"Now that you've brought up the other women, there must be someone in your life who'd go out of their way to please you.'' Not that she wanted to hear about them in detail, but if she wanted to get to know Jack better, his private life was important, too.

"None that count."

From his solemn tone she realized their time together meant more to him than a one-night stand and the notion pleased her. "If I can make you smile, that's enough for me."

"Which is exactly what I mean. You're beautiful inside and out. You just gave me proof of the first. And those incredible eyes of yours and well-kissed lips are proof of the second."

She dipped her head, unable to process the thrill that infused her, enjoyment and gratitude that wasn't merely sexual or egotistical in nature. "Thank you," she said simply.

"The pleasure was mine. But not *only* mine, I hope." He tilted his head in a cocky move she knew was meant to tease her.

She lifted a shaking hand to her mouth and his darkened gaze followed the movement. The man did know how to kiss. He also knew how to distract her from her plan and somehow this seduction had gotten away from her.

Despite all her preparation, *she* was the one being pleasured, and falling hard for Jack Latham, a caring man with whom she had no future. She rubbed a hand over her face as she accepted the long-term effects of this night.

She'd never see a beach again without thinking of Jack. Never inhale the warm fragrant scent of coconut oil without remembering how his hands gave her immense pleasure. And she'd never again glance in a mirror without remembering Jack and how he'd attempted to make up for every neglectful thing her parents had done by forcing her to view herself through his eyes.

He'd gone out of his way for her and she wanted to repay him. Besides, she needed to regain control. Of the situation, herself and her rampaging feelings.

"Did you really think I'd let you get away with only half your oil finished?" She reached for the bottle and waved it in the air. "It's almost time to hit the water." She gestured toward the sliding glass doors where the outside beckoned.

The sun had dipped well below the horizon and darkness had fallen. She knew from her prior night at the cabin that soon the beach would be completely deserted. They could share a moonlit walk uninterrupted. Or a nude swim, a wicked voice in her head taunted her.

Jack raised an eyebrow. "Far be it for me to deny you the pleasure."

She rolled her eyes and let out an exasperated groan. He was incorrigible.

Irresistible.

She crooked a finger his way. "Come here and learn all about that mirror you seem so fond of."

He met her on the bed with a half jump, half dive, rolled onto his back, arms spread wide. "I'm all yours, sweetheart."

She wished, she thought, and immediately stifled the sentiment. "On your stomach, head over here." She patted the end of the bed and he stretched out in front of her. He was tanned and muscular and he beckoned to the feminine part of her she'd spent years hiding away. She swung her leg around and settled herself astride his lower back. She bracketed his waist and his warm body heat shot from her thigh straight to her core.

He let out a low groan. ''Is this what they mean by exquisite torture?''

''I suppose it is.'' With a laugh, she squeezed her legs tighter.

She'd meant to tease him but ended up tormenting herself instead as a wave of longing swept through her. Each time she and Jack were together was deeper and more intimate than the last. She wondered if the control she so longed for would return, or if it was gone forever, along with her easy acceptance of being the office ice queen.

And of being alone.

She pushed reality aside for the moment. Summoning her courage, she braced her hands on his shoulders and shifted her hips in a circular motion.

Jack clenched his fingers around the comforter beneath him. Feeling Mallory's legs around his waist in a viselike grip was arousing him beyond belief. Her feminine heat, pressed hot and eager against his bare back, fed the desire. His erection pulsed into the mattress and his heart pounded hard in his chest.

He wanted to flip her over, lift her skirt, and bury himself in her hot, wet body. Problem was, he knew his emotions were too close to the surface and he'd be releasing far more than pent up sexual energy.

From the moment he'd retied her bathing suit and

glimpsed the sweet gratitude and desire in her face, something inside him softened and he didn't know how to repackage himself and his emotions so he was the Terminator once more. A man who felt nothing and needed nothing from the women in his life.

Seeking a distraction from the intense sensations Mallory aroused, Jack glanced into the mirror. Far from finding the diversion he sought, he found paradise. Thanks to the glass in front of him, not only could he feel the tightening of her thighs and the slight shift forward of her hips, but he could watch it as well.

Her body glistened from the coconut oil. He moved his gaze upward. Dark hair spilled over her shoulders, one long strand stuck against her cheek and her neck arched—but her eyes shone bright as she watched their movements in the mirror. Actually viewing the play of sexual pleasure cross her face as she rode astride him was carnal, arousing all his baser instincts. And when her gaze met his in the reflective glass, he was lost.

She reached for the bottle of oil and Jack knew he couldn't handle another massage without embarrassing himself in the process.

"What do you say we go for that swim?" His voice sounded ragged to his ears.

"Sounds great." She swung her legs to the side, seemingly all too eager to scramble off him and escape.

JACK AWOKE with a groan. He stretched, yawned and hit the floor for sit-ups before heading downstairs. But not even the morning sun shining into the restaurant helped to awaken him. Once again, he'd walked Mallory to her door across the hall from his, having separated by mutual agreement after their walk on the beach. His control had hung by a thread and he'd wanted to be with her more than he'd ever wanted another woman.

He should have just ceded control and satisfied the craving only she inspired. After all, what red-blooded man didn't attempt to go further with a woman he desired and one who responded in kind? A man who wanted the challenge to continue, that's who. That was one theory Jack could buy in to. It was the alternative that bugged him more.

Because the only other reason he would push her away was fear. Fear of getting in too deep—something he'd never worried about before—but he did now, with Mallory.

But not enough to stay away from her.

"We've got to stop meeting like this." He jumped as Mallory's soft voice whispered in his ear, catching him off guard.

He glanced over his shoulder as she walked around him and took her usual seat across from him. "I couldn't sleep so I went for a walk on the beach."

He took in her tailored pants, rolled into cuffs at the bottom and her light lavender oxford shirt. "Dressed like that?"

She shook her head and laughed. "Don't start."

"I wouldn't dare." Instead he leaned forward in his seat. "Did anyone ever tell you you look most sexy when you're not trying?"

The more he saw her in conservative mode, the more he liked and appreciated her contradictions. Far from wanting her to leave the conventional clothing behind, he'd begun to look forward to her daytime façade—because he knew he'd be the one to undress her at night.

"You shouldn't tease me in broad daylight." Her words were chiding but her voice was soft.

Before he could respond, he felt a brush of heat against his calf.

"Sorry."

"No problem." He shifted in his seat and swung his legs over to the other side. If she was going to play prim and proper, he didn't need mistaken touches beneath the table working to arouse him.

"So as long as I have appearances to keep up I would appreciate you not discussing it again."

He nodded.

"I appreciate your being so accommodating." She shut her mouth, pursed her lips in a look that reminded him of his grandmother and blew on the coffee before taking a sip.

He reached for his glass of water and downed half the contents. He suddenly felt another fleeting warmth stir against his leg. A second passed before it registered that her touch wasn't an accident but a deliberate caress of her foot against his bare leg.

He glanced up and caught her perusing the menu, but her lips were curled upward in a grin she couldn't contain.

She hooked one foot around his calf and pulled his legs apart, then settled her arch against his thigh. Her toes were dangerously close to hitting a bulls-eye and any semblance of control he'd mustered was almost gone.

"Mallory." Even he heard the warning edging his tone.

"Hmm?" She glanced up from the menu, wide-eyed but nowhere near innocent.

"What about those appearances you were talking about?" He grasped for a reminder of daily reality, anything to distract her wandering feet and his raging libido. But apparently appearances were all that concerned her because beneath the table where no one could see, her naughtier side had taken over.

She lifted her shoulders. "Look around you, Jack. No one's paying the least bit of attention to me. I've accomplished one of my goals."

An unexpected smile lit her face. "And now I'm about to accomplish another one." Her foot wiggled in a provocative movement designed to arouse and entice. And she did both well.

He couldn't speak without embarrassing himself with a full-fledged groan, and he couldn't shift positions without allowing her deeper, fuller access. So he settled for counting to himself and attempting to focus on anything but her tantalizing, stirring movements.

"Remember that tension you wouldn't let me relieve last night?" she purred.

He knew it all right. The same tension had built up inside him again, ready to explode and the little minx knew it.

"Good morning." Paul Lederman's booming voice

called out in the quiet dining room. "Mind if I join you?"

Jack couldn't answer if his life depended on it.

"Our pleasure," Mallory said, speaking for him. But she didn't remove her damn foot from its perch.

Jack shifted in his seat, unsuccessfully ignoring the push of her arch against his groin and the shot of white heat that followed in its wake.

He cleared his throat. "I hope you had a successful trip."

"The best kind." Lederman chose the seat beside Mallory, across from Jack.

At least Jack didn't have to worry about her leg hitting the wrong target, but he still needed breathing room or he'd detonate like a grenade.

"I'm looking into buying another resort. This one's in Nantucket," Lederman said.

Jack made a mental note to check with the firm's corporate and real estate partners to see what, if anything, they knew of this supposed deal.

He narrowed his eyes and gave Mallory a look that promised retribution. She averted her gaze.

"Nantucket's a beautiful location, or so I hear." She sat up straighter in her seat, in what would have been her professional attorney mode—were it not for her strategically placed foot.

"It's perfect," Lederman agreed.

"Speaking of perfect, I checked out the gym here. That's quite a setup you've got going." With Mallory having the upper hand, or in this case, the upper foot, on the family jewels, Jack decided not to mention Eva at the moment.

The older man nodded. "People who come here are looking to get away from stress. What with cell phones and laptop computers, most bring stress with them. The least a resort can provide is a full-service gym and a doctor on call."

Mallory fiddled with the spoon beside her empty plate before meeting their client's gaze. "Speaking of doctors, how have you been feeling, Mr. Lederman?"

The older man sucked in his stomach at the obviously unexpected question. "Never better, why do you ask?" His tone grew wary yet defensive at the same time.

Tread lightly, Jack thought. But he surprised himself by *not* jumping in to smooth things over between Mallory and their client—a sure sign he trusted her. Trusted Mallory or trusted her abilities? Jack would be a fool not to recognize the distinction, even if he couldn't accurately answer the question.

As quickly as she'd positioned herself, she eased her foot down and leaned forward in her seat. But Jack was quick enough to clamp his legs together and grab her by the ankle, leaving her at his mercy as she attempted to formulate a response.

In a move that surprised him, she took off her glasses, and propping her chin on her hand, she concentrated solely on Paul. "Please don't think I'm prying, but one of your employees mentioned you'd had a short stay in the hospital last year."

Surfer boy, Jack thought. He'd never gotten an answer about what she'd discovered the other night. How could he when he'd been too busy discovering *her?*

"Gossiping among the staff?" Lederman's expression grew thunderous.

She shook her head quickly back and forth. "Actually, no. It was raving by the staff. I'd mentioned how wonderful I thought the gym was—especially the doctor on call—you see my father had a mild heart attack recently..."

She trembled as she spoke and without thought, Jack clamped his legs tighter around her foot in the only display of comfort and support he could offer under the circumstances. It wasn't enough and for the first time, he wished he was free to express his feelings. And he realized he had some serious thinking to do when it came to Mallory Sinclair, colleague, and Mallory Sinclair, woman.

Her surprised gaze darted to his and in the blue depths he caught a glimmer of appreciation and a hint of calming. He took heart in knowing he'd been able to soothe her somehow.

Then she settled her gaze on Lederman who had begun patting her hand, and she went on. "So I thought your hotel would be a perfect getaway for my parents. They adore their time alone, but my mother would feel so much better knowing they could go on vacation where he could exercise under a doctor's supervision and she wouldn't have to watch over him."

Lederman visibly relaxed, the strain around his mouth easing as Mallory's story worked on him, no doubt as it was meant to.

Because Jack was already privy to her strained and unhappy relationship with her parents, he was not only sympathetic as Lederman was, but he needed to know more. Like how the heart attack—which he had no doubt was real—had affected Mallory's feelings toward her already distant parent. If that was the reason she was afraid to chart her own destiny instead of the one she thought would finally please her father and make him proud.

There was definitely more to this story than she'd revealed to Paul Lederman. More even than she'd revealed to Jack so far.

She smiled at Paul, batting those eyelashes behind the thick glasses she'd repositioned on her nose. "So you see, your employee was explaining how you upgraded the gym last year after your own trauma. And I have to say I'm impressed you were savvy enough to turn what had to be a traumatic experience into something so incredible."

Lederman, Jack had learned, was a sucker for compliments from younger women, and Mallory had obviously discovered the same thing. She was a pro at her job and played Lederman much the same way. Yet Jack sensed her sincerity, and it was the sincerity that calmed Lederman.

The older man beamed. "Young lady, you give your parents my name and I'll see to it they have a first-class stay here."

"Well thank you, Mr. Lederman."

He shook his head. "Paul."

"Thank you, Paul, but I wasn't fishing for anything from you. Honestly I was impressed with the facility and also concerned about your health."

The older man turned to Jack. "You've got a special lady working for you."

"I'll be sure to pass your compliments along," Jack said for Mallory's sake, knowing how important client impressions were in her bid for partner. "And remember, Paul, you'd be fortunate to have her on your side."

Mallory filled with warmth at Jack's easily spoken words. Though a part of her recognized his statement as a ploy to reinforce Waldorf, Haynes as Lederman's attorneys of choice, Jack's penetrating gaze held a wealth of meaning for her alone.

"I'm feeling much better, thank you," Lederman went on. "The gym's a part of my renewed health plan, and knowing I'll be free soon is another."

"Free to do what? You know you can tell us," she said, deliberately playful. Mallory wanted Lederman comfortable enough to reveal his secrets. The only reason she'd mentioned her father's recent heart scare at all was to gain his trust with an open revelation of her own.

Though she'd never admitted it aloud, the incident had thrown her badly. Instead of reinforcing her need to make partner before her father suffered more severe health problems, Mallory had seen the importance of enjoying life. When she'd begun to realize that she wasn't as fulfilled as she had thought she'd panicked and forced the issue from her mind, refusing to face her father's mortality and her dissatisfaction with the life she'd chosen.

Until now.

With Jack now in the equation, the thought of returning to the empty life she led back home loomed ominously before her.

Lederman's laughter boomed out in the quiet room. "See, I divulge my manly fantasies and she isn't even listening. Should I be insulted?"

Mallory flushed, realizing she'd been so engrossed in an internal monologue, she'd forgotten to pay attention to the more important things going on around her.

Jack laughed along with him. "Not at all. Even if she'd heard, you could still face her in the morning. Mallory's one of the boys."

If not for the distinct regret she caught flickering across Jack's face, she'd have reached across the table and strangled him in his seat. Mallory didn't care if Jack's statement had been made to solidify the bond and trust between the three of them.

No matter how good Jack's reasons, his words stung, harsher than the frigid comments he'd made on day one. Because he hadn't known her then, but he did now. More intimately than any other man ever had.

Or ever would again. She deliberately yanked her foot free from his hold, ignoring his icy glare.

"Ms. Sinclair?" The hostess stood by the edge of the table, portable phone in hand. "There's a call for you. You can take it outside." The young woman gestured to the balcony overlooking the water.

"Thank you." Mallory accepted the phone. "I've been expecting this. It's probably Rogers," she said to Jack, without mentioning the words private investigator in front of Lederman.

She wanted to see what the P.I. had dug up on Mrs. Lederman first before they showed their hand to Paul.

On a professional level Mallory agreed with Jack's philosophy about never going into a case unprepared yet her stomach cramped and she secretly hoped Rogers had come up empty. She hated the idea of digging for dirt on Mrs. Lederman, never mind how she'd feel if they actually found something useable.

At this moment, necessity didn't make her job any more appealing. "If you gentleman will excuse me?" She rose from her seat and both men stood.

She'd catch up with Jack later and fill him in on the call. As to whether anything else transpired between them—well the next invitation was up to him.

11

JACK WATCHED Mallory's retreat, regret clenching and unclenching his gut. Calling her one of the boys had been necessary, but one of the hardest things he'd ever done—because he knew how deep his words would wound her. There was nothing he could do about it now, so he turned back to Lederman.

"Come on, Paul, she's gone. Now tell me what you've got going. I met up with Eva down at the gym. Now she's hot."

"She's yesterday. You know that Nantucket deal I was telling you about?" He dropped his voice to a hushed tone.

Jack groaned. "Don't tell me you're buying a resort just to get an in with some woman." He glanced out toward the large veranda-like porch where Mallory had gone and realized he'd buy a lot more than land just to keep her with him.

The more he learned about her past, the better he understood her. He respected her professional climb and he trusted her.

"What better way to retain control of the situation?" Lederman asked.

Jack sighed. Regardless if he could empathize with the concept Lederman had just broached, professionally the man was talking a suicide move. Paul was thinking but not with his brain.

"Look, say you hire me and I get you out of this marriage with most of your assets intact. Why would you go buying yourself a problem? Screw the woman if you have to and walk away. You've heard of sexual harassment. You buy the resort, you're buying yourself major headaches."

"This woman's special." The older man leaned forward in his seat. "And she understands me, something I don't have now."

"They're all special in the beginning," Jack said, repeating the same mantra he'd used on other clients embarking on an affair while embroiled in a messy divorce.

Only this time, a voice in his head he'd never heard before argued that maybe Lederman had a point. Maybe one woman *could* be special enough to make it worth risking everything for.

That's when Jack knew morning or not, he needed a stiff drink. Or an immediate getaway from the enclosed hotel atmosphere and the intensity of the feelings Mallory effortlessly invoked.

Lederman shook his head, his lips thinning in disappointment. "You're too young to be so cynical. Maybe you need to get lucky yourself."

Jack let out a laugh. Lederman would fall over in his chair if he knew how close Jack was to getting lucky. "You're paying me to be cynical. Which reminds me, are we in or out as your divorce attorneys? Because much as I like it here, I can't afford to lounge around much longer."

"Relax, Jack. Like you said, I'm paying you to lounge around. I'll see you later."

Jack groaned. What he needed was to get the hell out of this resort and back into the real world, but with Lederman calling the shots that wouldn't be happening. Still, there were other ways of alleviating his cabin fever.

The ball was back in his court where Mallory was concerned, and he knew just the solution. He'd take Mallory into the real world—where he'd see how little they had in common and where he'd be reminded of how much he hated the feeling of being tied to any one woman.

Special ones like Mallory included.

MALLORY STOOD in the luxury gift shop of the hotel, looking over the array of eyewear. She tried on gold-rimmed Fendi frames, thick-framed black Gucci sunglasses and Prada glasses with no frames at all. They were all way out of her price range, but she continued to look, convinced that wearing such feminine and sexy glasses would rebuild her pride, still wounded from being called one of the boys. By Jack.

"Have you made a decision?" The saleswoman asked.

Mallory shook her head. "I'd love these." She slid on the Prada glasses, so opposite of her daily frames, and posed in front of the mirror. With the sun shining through the windows and no heavy black lenses bogging her down she felt lighter and freer.

"The lavender tint compliments your skin tone."

Mallory didn't know if that was truth or a sales

pitch, not that it mattered. "Unfortunately they're beyond my means." She'd spent her surplus money on the cozy cabin for herself and Jack. The memories they made there would last a lot longer than an expensive pair of sunglasses or the illusion of femininity and freedom they provided.

All she needed to do was glance in the mirror without her glasses to see the shabby truth. She pulled off the shades and handed them back to the woman. "Thank you anyway."

"My pleasure. Here's my card if you change your mind."

Mallory smiled. "I appreciate that." She left the store, realizing she'd fallen into an *oh-poor-me* routine that was as pathetic as it was unnecessary.

She'd chosen her life and had no business regretting it now, just because she'd gone and fallen in love with Jack.

She'd fallen in love with Jack.

Mallory stumbled toward the group of chairs arranged in the center of the lobby. She settled herself into the nearest one before her knees buckled beneath her. *She'd fallen in love with Jack.* The revelation shouldn't be a shock. It was exactly what she'd feared when she'd embarked on this trip, even though she hadn't voiced that fear aloud. Her heart thudded hard in her chest. She tried to calm herself by forcing deep and even breaths.

She'd get through this. For once her past was going to work in her favor. If she could learn to live without the love of her parents, she could darn well learn to live without Jack's.

"Excuse me, Miss?"

At the sound of the saleswoman's voice, Mallory turned around. "Are you calling me?"

The blond-haired woman nodded. "These are for you." She held out a sunglass case with the silver Prada logo on top.

Mallory shook her head. "I don't understand."

"A good-looking man with dark hair said to tell you there's a note inside. You are so lucky. It's such a romantic gesture."

"Well…" Speechless, Mallory accepted the case. As the saleswoman retreated, Mallory stayed seated so she could read and absorb Jack's words.

What good are sunglasses without a convertible? Join me for the ride of your life. Fifteen minutes out front. If you dare to go out in broad daylight.

She slipped the glasses on and her adrenaline started pumping. Mallory Sinclair wasn't a quitter. She wasn't someone who felt sorry for herself and wallowed in pity. She was a survivor who made the best of what life threw her way.

But for whatever time they had left, fate had given her Jack. She loved him and maybe she couldn't have him for forever—but she could most definitely have him for now.

MALLORY MANAGED to change clothes and get back downstairs with one minute to spare. She walked outside, caught sight of the red convertible gleaming in the sunlight and fell in love—this time with the sleek machine and the lure of freedom. Not to mention the man sitting in the driver's seat.

He was tanned and sexy and waiting just for her. He honked the horn and waved her over. "Come on before we miss the best part of the day."

She couldn't see his eyes behind his darkened shades but just looking at him warmed her blood faster than the sun overhead. She ran to the car and jumped into the passenger seat. She paused only to pull her new glasses out of her bag and slide them onto the bridge of her nose. "I won't ask how you knew about these but thank you just the same."

He slung one arm over the back of her seat. "You're welcome. Pleasing you is my number one priority."

"Ooh, I like the sound of that." She rubbed her hands together and reminded herself he was joking. "Where are we going?"

He grinned. "You'll see."

She kicked her sandals off and curled her legs beneath her. "I can't wait."

He studied her intently. His admiring gaze never left her face. "You look sexy in those lenses."

She couldn't doubt his sincerity and the compliment soothed her bruised feelings from earlier. "Thank you."

His fingers brushed her bare shoulders, skimming the flesh her halter exposed, and she trembled. "That top is something else, too. Or should I say it's the body beneath it that's so spectacular."

She laughed. "You can say whatever you want as long as you keep those compliments coming."

"That's no hardship, sweetheart."

Her heart lodged in her throat. She couldn't let his

sweet-talking words go to her head. "Don't you think we ought to get going before someone sees us looking and acting less than businesslike?"

"As usual you've got a point." He shifted gears into drive, put his foot to the pedal and they hit the road. "And speaking of business, what's going on with Rogers?"

Mallory shrugged. "He thinks he's onto something. He'll be in touch."

"Soon, I hope. Lederman's stalling is making me crazy. John Waldorf says things at the office are status quo and they're handling his most recent business— no mention of Nantucket but it may be too new. We'll see."

She nodded. "But it's all moot for the day anyway."

"So let's put it behind us for now, yes?"

She grinned. "Yes." A day alone with Jack. She could handle that.

She'd let down her hair for his benefit and as the car picked up speed, the warm wind blew the longer pieces wildly around her face. She reveled in the freedom as he drove with one hand and laced his fingers through the strands with the other.

The sensual tugging on her scalp felt wickedly good. She leaned her head against the seat, shut her eyes and gave herself over to the sensation of the wind and his hands playing a seductive dance in her hair and against her skin.

"This is heaven," she said aloud.

"Just wait till we reach our destination."

Almost forty minutes of bliss and comfortable silence later they turned onto a road that ran parallel to the beach and boasted huge estates on the water.

Mallory peered through her sunglasses at the mansions, replete with gates, security systems and too many rooms to possibly count. Each one had a magnificent view. With the sun high in the blue sky and not a cloud in sight, the water seemed to go on forever.

Leaning closer to him for a better view out his side, his potent, masculine scent assaulted her senses. It was all she could do not to cuddle close. Thank heavens for the gear shift, she thought, which protected her from her baser impulses.

"Did you ever wonder what it would be like to live in one of those homes?" she asked instead.

His grunt let her know exactly what he thought of that question. "I grew up in a two-bedroom apartment in the city. One of those places was never within the realm of possibility." His jaw clenched, making her think she'd hit a nerve.

She quickly changed the subject. "Well, I grew up in the suburbs. We used to go to Cape Cod and Rhode Island for a few weeks during the summers—as soon as sleep-away camp ended, which was how they got rid of me during the bulk of the summer."

She shifted in her seat and glanced out the window at the ocean beyond. "My parents would drop me at an aunt's house while they took off shopping or sightseeing. *'You stay home, Mallory. You're too young to appreciate antiques,'*" she said in a perfect imitation of her mother.

"She sounds charming."

"Cool is more like it. They both were. After dropping me off, they'd take these romantic drives around the beach or into town. I know this because it's all my mother would talk about when they finally got back hours later—sometimes days if the whim struck."

His assessing eyes bore into hers before he turned his focus back to the road. "You hated being left out."

She gripped her forearms tight, hugging herself against the memories that surfaced as hard and strong as the ocean current. "I hated being the third wheel, which I was whether I was dragged along with them or left behind."

"How'd you get through it?"

"By daydreaming about living in a castle or fantasy house where everyone catered to what *I* wanted. Especially my parents who couldn't bear to be separated from their only daughter." She let out a cynical laugh. "As if."

His gut clenched in her defense. *As if* anything he felt on her behalf could chase away the truth of that awful time in her life. He hated that anyone could make her feel so isolated and alone.

"And now? You mentioned a heart scare to Lederman. Did you get through it okay?"

She leaned her head back against the seat. "It was easy enough to get through the incident itself considering they never called me until after he was released from the hospital and only then because they were returning *my* call. As usual they forgot all about me."

Jack winced. He had wanted to protect her from

the pain, not dig into old wounds. "I didn't mean to pry."

She laughed, easing the tension. "Sure you did, but that's okay. I didn't mean to bore you with my life story."

"You could never bore me." Anything that gave him an inkling as to what made her the woman she'd become was a fascination for him.

"Yeah and I own some of this beachfront property I could sell you dirt cheap." She grinned and the arousal he'd somehow held at bay for the entire drive came rushing back in full force.

He could see the sparkle in her eyes even behind the dark glasses and her easy smile seemed meant for him alone. Even if it wasn't, he wouldn't mind deluding himself for a while longer. But at least her quick comeback told him she underestimated the effect she had on him—which was a good thing since it afforded him some protection against falling too hard.

And maybe he had some beachfront property he could sell himself, he thought wryly. He eased the car into a slow crawl. "Any more dreams you want to share? Like the ones for your future?"

"You mean, do I have the American dream of being someone's wife with the house, the white picket fence, kids and a dog? Or do I dream of being barefoot and pregnant running around the kitchen baking cake and organizing PTA meetings?" She let out an ineloquent snort. "Not hardly."

He propped one arm over the wheel and studied the woman beside him. Sarcasm aside, he caught a wistful quality in her voice and the longing in her expression told him she wanted some of those things more than she let on. Maybe even more than she admitted to herself.

And despite all good intentions, he could envision her in either of those roles she'd mentioned because Mallory was a woman who could accomplish anything she chose. When it came to the barefoot and pregnant part, well he was certain she'd excel at the getting pregnant part.

The driving need to test his theory grew stronger. So did the erection inside his shorts. It was a wonder she hadn't called him on it already.

"What no comment? The Terminator has nothing to say on my feelings about the American family?" she asked.

He felt sure she didn't want to know what he was thinking at the moment. He donned a grin. "The Terminator doesn't believe in the American dream either."

She clucked her tongue. "I didn't say I don't believe, I said it won't be happening for me. I'm the dreamer, remember?"

He nodded. "Dreams are for people who haven't experienced reality." Not wanting to get caught up in the fantasy, he brushed it off as easily as she'd pretended to.

"What's your reality, Jack? It seems to me I've exposed my soul while yours is still hidden."

Knowing she had a point, he said, "My parents' marriage was, or should I say is, the opposite of your folks'."

"I'm sorry."

He shrugged. "Nothing to apologize for. It is what it is."

"Doesn't sound that simple to me. Take it from someone who knows. These things stay with you."

His chest constricted, knowing she'd unintentionally struck him where it hurt. "I'm sure you're right."

"Does your choice in careers have anything to do with what you saw growing up?"

He shook his head. "I fell into family law." He started to give her the same rehearsed speech he'd given many times before when he suddenly changed his mind. "Actually, it has everything to do with it." He reached out and stroked one finger down her thigh, toying with the fringe on her cut-off shorts.

She covered his hand with hers, stilling his intentionally distracting movements. Her warmth soothed him and he was able to continue. "At first I figured I'd become a lawyer and get my father out of the hell his marriage had become."

"And then?" she asked quietly.

"Then I realized he stuck around because on some level he liked the sick situation, or was too weak to get out of it on his own. By then I had a career and was on that partnership track you know so well. I wasn't giving that up so…here I am."

"The Terminator."

"Yup. Meanwhile my folks are still married and making each other miserable." They inched along the road parallel to the beach. And as they continued to drive in silence, Jack realized that admitting those truths out loud for the first time gave him a sense of freedom he'd never had.

"You told me why your father stuck around, but why hasn't your mother opted out?"

"Because my mother doesn't know the meaning of fidelity, and since my father doesn't know how to stand up for himself and get the hell out, she's got the best of both worlds."

At least she had until now. Jack still didn't know if his father would go through with the divorce.

"That's sad. And so opposite of my parents. Which I guess goes to show you that neither extreme is a healthy one."

"Guess not." He shrugged, not knowing what else to say.

He inhaled the salty ocean air. He'd never spoken about his family life before, but he trusted his past in Mallory's hands.

And he needed those hands around him now. Badly.

"So you shut down your dreams for the future, afraid you'll end up the same way?" she asked.

"It would seem so." He shouldn't be surprised she hadn't passed judgment, merely understood.

But those dreams she thought he'd shut down were pushing past the barriers he'd built, and they centered around Mallory, threatening the stability and peace he thought he'd found.

He glanced her way. The sunglasses he'd seen her eyeing earlier were perched on her scrunched-up nose. The wind had blown her hair into wild disarray and her cheeks were flushed from being outdoors—

just how he imagined she'd look after a hot night of making love. With him.

Damn. Why hadn't he thought of it as just sex? Jack swallowed back a curse. Had he really thought getting away from the hotel would give him distance? All this trip had done was bring them closer emotionally. This getaway hadn't made him want her any less nor had it alleviated the burning tension inside him.

"And those dreams of yours. Are they shut down as well?" he asked.

She nodded. "I got older, immersed myself in reality, decided to follow in my father's footsteps and try to make the old man proud."

"That's too bad. Because I have a hunch if you let yourself, you'd find a goldmine of untapped dreams inside you."

She rested her chin on bended knee and glanced his way. "Maybe I was wrong." Her expression grew pensive. "I don't think anyone can really close themselves off to dreaming," she said softly. "Including you."

He would have vehemently disagreed before this trip. He hadn't thought he had any dreams for the future beyond the life he'd created. He'd always associated women with his mother and marriage with his parents' disaster of a union.

And now...

"What was I thinking?" she asked before he could take his thoughts any further. "Macho men don't dream and if they do, they don't admit it." She laughed, breaking the seriousness that had been surrounding them.

The sound, light and carefree, eased the growing knot of tension in his stomach. She was back to relaxing. Best of all she wasn't asking him for a damn thing beyond their stolen time together. So why was he allowing himself to get caught up in such serious considerations like relationships, marriage and the future?

He turned his attention to the scenery. They'd left the stretch of homes behind and the now empty beach stretched out before them. Jack spotted a deserted outlet beneath a boardwalk where he could park. He turned into a secluded spot that afforded them a perfect view of the water, and because they were still in an exclusive area, they wouldn't be interrupted by tourists. Jack silently thanked Eva, the gym manager, for telling him about this place even though her reasons for helping him would make Mallory green with jealousy.

He shifted to park and before he could blink she climbed over the seat and into the back, motioning for him to join her.

He studied her and glanced around them. "You sure about this?"

"Are you afraid of getting caught?"

He flew out of the car and joined her in the back seat. "You're naughty, Mallory. And you're also forgetting who extended this invitation." He pulled her into his arms and into the kiss he'd been dying for all afternoon.

She didn't resist. Her lips opened wide and she let

him in, deeper than he'd thought possible. He moved his mouth over hers, tasting her luscious lips before moving to nuzzle her cheek, lingering only seconds before traveling down to her neck.

He suckled and soothed, then inhaled the fragrant scent of her perfume. "Man, you smell good."

"Then keep going." She tilted her head to provide him with better access as he slid his wet tongue across her collarbone. He pulled on the neck of her shirt and pressed butterfly-light kisses to the white skin on the swell of her breast.

She shuddered and let out a trembling sigh, but caught him off guard when her hands moved to the fly on his shorts. His brain warned him to stop as he had last night, but this time he couldn't. He'd been holding back for too long, needed release by her hands too badly.

The pop of the snap echoed in the car and the rasp of his zipper moving over his straining erection caused a surge of renewed desire to flood his veins. "Sweetheart, our first time is not going to be in the back seat of an open convertible," he said.

She opened her mouth to reply.

He pressed one finger to her lips. "Hush. Because nothing you say now, including a challenge is going to change my mind."

She licked at his finger and a sizzling current traveled from her hot mouth straight to his groin. He clenched his fists and cocked his head to the side.

"Okay. I can play just as easily another way." She pushed his legs apart in a wide vee and settled herself inbetween before dropping to her knees in front of him.

Her hands reached for the band of his shorts and he let out a strangled groan.

"Lift your hips."

He liked the command and his waist bucked forward in an involuntary response.

Mallory laughed. "That's not what I meant."

The strain of desire was wearing on him. "I know what you meant. I just can't believe you mean to do this here."

Her blue eyes darkened with real passion. "Oh, but I do." She reached for the blanket on the floor beside her. He'd bought it in the gift shop, in case they stopped for food and wanted to sit on the beach. "Good planning, wouldn't you say?" she asked.

"It's not the reason I bought it."

She shrugged. "That's okay. I won't hold it against you if my imagination's better than yours. It's a female thing I guess." She wiggled her eyebrows. "Now lift those hips."

"Bossy wench."

"Yeah, and you love it."

Damn but she was right. He glanced around. Not a single person or car was in sight for what seemed like miles. But just in case he spread the blanket wide and tossed it over the headrest of the front seat. "Just in case."

She giggled. "You can cover me and your lower half if you need to."

He rolled his eyes. "And explain what I'm doing

alone in the back seat of a car covered by a blanket in the heat of the day.''

"You're a smart man. I'm sure you'll think of something."

In another minute he figured he'd be too far gone to utter a coherent word. He raised his hips off the seat and helped her wrest his shorts down to his ankles, freeing his erection for her waiting hands.

She didn't waste a minute. As he watched, she cupped his length in her delicate fingers, which were warmer and stronger than they looked. His body shook and he leaned his head back and exhaled a groan.

"Watch me, Jack."

He opened his eyes. She'd pay later for this control thing of hers, but right now he liked her being in charge too much to do anything about it except enjoy.

So he watched.

Just as she lowered her head and licked at him with her tongue. "Oh, man." The words burst from him as his hips thrust forward and he nearly came right then.

"I'm assuming that's a good thing?" She raised her head and asked lightly, but he sensed the import of her words.

That she didn't do this often filled him with ridiculous male pride. That she did it now, for him, filled him with a sweeping emotion so strong he didn't dare give it a name. Not that he could have because at that moment she took him into her warm, wet, willing mouth and Jack was lost.

Her hands worked a slick vertical gliding motion

in synchronized rhythm with her talented mouth. If he was an experiment, she'd found the formula for success. His hips began a gyrating motion he couldn't control, bucking up and down without regard to her sensual assault.

She licked and suckled, providing friction with her tongue. She pulled and pushed with her slick palms, bringing him to the peak and easing him back without allowing him the pleasure of release.

"Mallory, please—" The word burst from him in a groan. He'd never begged a woman before. But this was Mallory, and experienced or not, she was so damn good.

Without warning, her hand position changed and she pressed at the base of his penis, in a spot low and deep. "Jesus, don't stop." She didn't and white-hot darts of fire exploded in every nerve ending he possessed.

Seconds before he came, he leaned forward and pulled her up and on top of him until her feminine heat aligned with his hot and ready erection.

She caught on quick, clamping her thighs tight around his and grinding her pelvis into his erection. He jerked his hips upward one last time and found the hottest, sweetest release he'd ever known.

Without being cocooned inside Mallory's warm body, it wasn't enough but at least when he came she was where she belonged, sitting on his lap and writhing against him, straining for her own release and helping the quaking shudders to continue wracking his body long after they should have ceased.

He closed his mouth over hers and with his palm,

he cupped her hard between the juncture of her thighs. She moaned and arched into his hand.

"That's it, sweetheart. Let me feel it." With his fingers, he worked her the best he could through the denim barrier and her hips gyrated in time to the movement of his hands.

"Harder, more, Jack please...please..." Her breathless words caused a renewed stirring in his loins and when she started to convulse against his hand, the sounds and the feelings were as strong and intense as his own orgasm.

She collapsed against him, her chest against his damp one, her head cradled in his shoulder and her breath hot and heavy in his ear.

MALLORY TRIED to move and couldn't. "I can't catch my breath."

His hands tangled in her hair. "I can't say that's a problem considering the reason."

She chuckled. "Good point." She'd meant to please him and she obviously had. He'd pleased her, too, but an aching emptiness in her body remained and Mallory understood the reason only too well. She hadn't experienced *everything* he had to give.

She'd had that same thought as she'd changed from her plain gray dress into the shorts and halter top she now wore. And she'd planned ahead.

"Jack?" She pushed herself back so she could meet his gaze.

Still clouded with residual desire, his dark eyes stared back at her. "What is it?"

"I hope you realize we're not finished yet."

Laughing, he leaned his head back against the leather seats and ran a hand through his hair. "I'm pretty damn well spent."

She punched him lightly in the shoulder. "That's not what I mean."

Though she had no intention of getting all weepy or clingy with a man who only took commitment seriously when it came to escaping one, she did plan to make her point.

She reached for her purse on the front seat of the car and pulled a silk scarf from the outside zipper.

"I draw the line at wearing women's clothing." His lips twitched in a grin.

She let out a breathless laugh. "Thank goodness."

His impossibly shaded eyes darkened as his palm caressed her calf.

A renewed stirring surged inside her. "Not yet."

She took the scarf and wrapped it around his neck like a tie, pulling down on the ends until he leaned forward, his lips inches from hers.

"Bring this to my room tonight," she ordered.

A wicked expression crossed his features, anticipation lighting his eyes. "Not the cabin?"

"I'd like to say it's already rented but the truth is I'm tapped out. But trust me, you don't need the cabin for what I have planned." She pressed her lips against his and teased him with a kiss that tantalized but her tongue never plunged into the warm recesses of his mouth.

"You're killing me." His lips moved against hers. "Now why would I do that before we've gone all the way?'' She wriggled her hips downward, feeling him begin to harden and swell beneath her.

''You feel good.''

''There's so much more where that came from. And remember, control is an illusion. Now be at my room at eight.'' She bolted for the front seat before her desire and feelings for this man overwhelmed her too soon.

12

MALLORY LAY on her bed staring into space. When she'd pleased Jack today, she'd done so knowing she loved him. When she made love with him tonight, she'd know the same. And with each step, she'd find it harder to walk away.

What had started as a game was now an important part of her life—memories she would store and treasure for always. The fun they'd shared and the feeling of having him inside her. And, she thought, recalling the scarf she'd grabbed from her drawer earlier in the day, she wanted to create those same memories for him as well.

She didn't want him to ever forget Mallory Sinclair. Because she knew for certain she'd never forget him.

She had only a few hours to prepare her room and herself. A tremor of excitement shimmied through her as she undressed, removing the clothing she'd worn for their trip today. A hot shower, a quick dinner and some last-minute arrangements and she'd be ready for Jack.

A hard knock on the door startled her. ''Coming.'' She slipped into her robe then glanced into the peephole.

"Jack?" Something had to be wrong, she thought, as she unlatched the chain.

She hadn't planned on seeing him until tonight.

She opened the door quickly. "What's wrong?"

His jaw was pulled tight with obvious tension and unease. "I need to make a quick trip back to the city," he said.

"Is everything okay?" She gestured with a sweep of her arm and he followed her inside. The door slammed shut behind them, enclosing them in the small entry to the room.

"Family emergency." He leaned back against the beige wall and shoved his hands into trouser pockets. His steely eyes were as cool as his voice.

Icy tentacles of unease swept through her. Mallory knew better than to take his change in attitude personally but his aloof demeanor hurt just the same. She curled her fingers into a fist to prevent herself from acting on impulse and smoothing the crease in his forehead or massaging the tension from his tight muscles.

He didn't seem as if he'd be receptive to any intimate gesture right now and considering how hard her heart was pounding in her chest, she doubted she could handle an outright rejection.

Not when she wanted desperately to ease his distress. So much for professionalism and remaining detached, she thought wryly. Falling in love had a way of shattering that kind of objectivity.

She clenched the lapels of her robe tighter in her hand. "I appreciate you letting me know."

"I didn't want to just disappear on you without an explanation."

Somewhere in the depths of his eyes, she sensed a softening of emotion and hoped she wasn't just imagining things she wanted to see. Though disappointment flowed heavy through her veins, so did concern. Whatever this family emergency was, it had changed his mood and affected him deeply.

She wondered if the urgency had to do with his parents but thought better of asking. If he wanted to confide in her he would. "When do you need to go?"

He glanced at his watch. "A car's picking me up in fifteen minutes."

Uncertain of what to say next, she clenched and unclenched her fingers around her robe. "Is there anything I can do?" she asked, finally.

He shook his head. "Just keep an ear out around here."

"I expect to hear from Rogers soon."

He nodded. "I'll check in with you when I get back."

She sensed he was too distracted to concentrate on business. "When do you think that will be?"

"I'm hoping to catch the last plane back tonight." He turned and placed one hand on the doorknob.

She didn't know why this felt like such a final goodbye but the possibility freed her to act on impulse. Mallory reached out and touched his shoulder. "Jack, wait."

He paused.

"I'll be here when you get back." She didn't feel the need to elaborate.

They'd been too close for him to misunderstand her meaning.

He turned. His hand covered hers, easing her clenched fist loose until her arm dropped to her side. "It's been my experience that women always want something."

She stiffened at his words, but forced herself to see his side. Watching constant infidelity had jaded him, she thought sadly, as she realized exactly why he held himself back from relationships and trust.

"I wonder what's on your agenda?" he asked.

Though she'd steeled herself for the verbal barb it stung anyway. Since *she'd* approached *him* with the first invitation, and since she had an overt agenda where work was concerned, she could see why he'd be searching for an ulterior motive now.

Yet the heart she'd lost to this man wished he could see inside her and not have to ask. She'd shared enough to give him twenty-twenty vision—if he cared to see.

She held herself upright and looked him straight in the eye. "Not a thing. Especially not partnership if that's what you're thinking. I could have gotten your support with less risk if I hadn't issued that first invitation."

She forced a smile to curve her lips, wanting to soften his mood and convince him that she cared only for his feelings, no other agenda in mind.

It worked. The painful distance in his gaze lessened, replaced by a surprising warmth instead. A fluttering heat rose in her belly, accompanied by a deeper more intense wash of feeling.

"True." His thumb brushed over her bottom lip.

Despite the earlier tension, a moist dewiness settled between her legs, a testament to the yearning he made her feel.

His gaze never left hers. "So what do you want, Mallory?" Curiosity melded with desire in his smoky depths.

"You," she said truthfully. Honestly. With more candor than she'd ever intended to provide. "I want you and I want your trust."

His hand cupped her chin, tipping her head upward. "I can promise you the first." Desire remained potent and strong, hovering between them. "No one gets my trust."

And from the determined look in his eyes, Mallory knew he wanted to believe his words. But she also knew how fast and hot the emotions poured between them.

If he needed her on his return, he knew where to find her. But if he showed up on her doorstep, he best be prepared. She thrived on a challenge and Jack had just thrown down a gauntlet she couldn't resist.

Not with the man she loved.

MALLORY MADE her way to the dining room, a paperback in her shoulder bag. She planned to eat a light dinner but she had an ulterior motive as well. With Jack gone, she had a prime opportunity to listen carefully for information on Lederman and poke around if she got the chance.

She'd finished her turkey wrap and soda and was about to call it a night when she caught sight of Alicia

Lederman walking into the restaurant. Though Mallory kept her book open, she made eye contact and hoped Alicia approached her first.

There was no way Mallory could instigate a sit-down meeting with Lederman's wife for a chat, but she certainly wouldn't be rude enough to walk away if the other woman sought her out first.

As the older woman made her way into the room, she glanced around, taking in her surroundings, and Mallory guessed, assessing the restaurant's customers and the staff's preparations for the evening. She had a hunch her client's wife had a hand in running things and the settlement wouldn't be as simple as Mr. Lederman hoped.

Alicia's gaze lit on Mallory. Instead of breaking eye contact Mallory held Alicia's stare until the other woman had no choice but to look away...or walk over to the table.

She chose the latter. "I trust you enjoyed your meal?" Alicia asked.

Mallory nodded. "Excellent. You have a very diverse menu."

"I worked with the chef myself." The other woman paused a beat. "Would you mind if I joined you?"

Without showing her pleasure, Mallory shook her head. "Not at all. But you were advised to deal with your own attorneys." She'd begun to care for the older woman and so she felt an obligation to see that Alicia looked out for her own interests.

"When the time is right I will." Alicia pulled out

a chair and seated herself across from Mallory. "Coffee?" She gestured to a waitress.

Mallory nodded. "Thank you."

"Did you know my daughter's in law school?" The older woman tucked a strand of short brown hair behind her ear.

"No I didn't. Does she enjoy it?"

She smiled. "She's not sure yet."

"Then it sounds like she's got a level head on her shoulders." Mallory laughed. "Make sure you tell her law school was memorable but not an indicator of real life."

"True." Alicia nodded as she toyed with a silver spoon. "But then what is?"

Mallory read the meaning behind the words and knew they were talking about more than life in general. "I can't imagine you're having an easy time." She felt compelled to acknowledge the other woman's anguish.

Pain darkened Alicia's brown eyes to a deeper, sadder shade. "I'm sure you can't imagine. And I mean no insult. But I'm talking about nearly twenty-five years of marriage. Of partnership. I never dreamed it would end on a whim." She clutched at a menu lying on the table with both hands, turning her knuckles white.

Her gestures communicated more clearly than her words, and Mallory made yet another mental note of Alicia's sincere anguish regarding her marriage.

"You feel you had a solid partnership?" Mallory felt compelled to ask.

Alicia shook her head. "Make no mistake, I knew

my husband's faults as well as my own but I did believe we could overcome anything. In fact I thought we once had.''

Mallory looked into the older and wiser woman's eyes. Despite her obvious pain, Alicia maintained that strength of character and resolve Mallory admired. "You still believe that, don't you?"

"If you love someone, you want to trust them. You want them to trust you."

Mallory immediately thought of Jack. How could she not when the last few days with him revolved around that very word. Trust.

"And," Alicia continued, oblivious to Mallory's inner thoughts, "you want to believe that if you trust in each other you can get through *anything* and be together forever."

She bowed her head and her shoulders dropped.

"But no matter how much I want to believe, I've got my eyes open. I'll look out for me if it comes to that. But I know what we shared was solid even if Paul has changed." Alicia leaned back in her seat. "Have you ever been in love?"

"No. No time." Mallory answered quickly before she could reveal her heart to this kind woman. And before she could let her mind wrap around the twin concepts Alicia had linked together. Love. Trust. And forever.

"Then you're missing out on life's greatest pleasure. I can tell you that with no regrets, even if I do end up divorced. You're too young and pretty to waste your life on the practice of law at the expense of everything else." The woman's eyes shone with certainty—the knowledge of a woman who'd loved and been loved.

Though Mallory ought to think of Alicia as her adversary, she'd been unable to sever the emotional connection she felt toward her. The woman had a warm, caring nature that Mallory was drawn to. But she wasn't surprised. With her own mother a parent in name only, it was hardly surprising that Mallory connected with a mature older woman who both sought and gave confidences and understanding.

Only after Alicia had patted her hand and walked away did Mallory realize she'd blown her chance at questioning their client's wife—in favor of a motherly chat and a lesson in love.

JACK RUBBED his eyes and inhaled deeply. His family emergency wasn't over yet, but he'd managed to calm his father down and convince him to let Jack drive him to his sister's house in Connecticut. Leave it to Jack's mother to show up to pack her things with current boyfriend in tow.

Jack leaned his head against the seat in the car he'd hired to take him back to the hotel.

His parents' marriage fell into the category he'd once described to Mallory. Two people who had stayed together out of convenience. His father couldn't imagine not being married to the woman he thought he loved, though Jack had a difficult time believing anything remained of the love the older man had once felt for his wife. His father just didn't have what it took to stand up for himself. His mother found it equally as convenient to sleep around without relinquishing the financial benefits and security the marriage provided.

Just growing up in their home, watching the two of them coexist while living their separate lives had aged Jack before his time and made him cynical. After all he'd seen and heard in his youth and later in his career, he couldn't share Mallory's optimistic view of marriage or even relationships. She might not think she wanted those things for herself, but he admired her for hanging on to her starry views.

More than likely some man would come along and sweep her off her feet. Jack only hoped she'd be able to maintain the faith, and that same man wouldn't disappoint her and shatter her illusions.

He hoped like hell *he* wouldn't be that man.

Because as much as his brain told him to head straight to his hotel room and get some sleep, as the car came to a stop outside the luxury hotel, he knew without a doubt he wouldn't be sleeping alone.

He slipped his hand into his pocket and pulled out Mallory's black scarf, a reminder of what awaited him when he got through this latest family trauma.

Mallory. She hadn't asked too many questions, but in a calm voice filled with understanding she had said she'd be there when he got back. Jack, a man who didn't believe in trust, took her at her word. He had no choice. Need had been building inside him all day. Not just desire, but an escalating need for one woman.

For her.

Given all he'd just witnessed between his parents, he should be more alarmed by the realization. He told himself it was because he knew there'd be no long-term fallout from their liaison. She knew the facts as well as he.

So why was he finding it harder and harder to believe the mantra he'd lived by his entire adult life?

Jack signed the car receipt and entered the quiet hotel lobby. He passed the closed shops and the bored desk clerk and headed up the elevator. The trip to the fifth floor took mere seconds but the ride stretched long like the coiled band of desire wracking his body.

He raised his fist, surprised to see his hand shaking. His frenzied state had less to do with worry over whether she'd turn him away than it did with pure unadulterated desire.

Jack leaned against the doorframe and waited. His heart pounded so loudly inside his chest he felt certain Mallory could hear it in her room. In the past when he'd overheard arguments between his parents or watched with silent frustration as his father accepted more than any man should, Jack had no outlet for the emotions pouring through him.

He had that outlet now. His gut told him Mallory wouldn't turn him away.

Drawing a deep breath he knocked on the door.

MALLORY KNEW without looking who stood on the other side of the closed door. And once she pulled the door open wide, she realized he wasn't here in response to her invitation as much as he was here because he needed to be.

The blankness she'd seen in his eyes earlier had been replaced by an emotion she'd never seen there before, a need so strong and intense it caused her entire body to shake in reaction.

"Hi." He leaned against the doorframe, outwardly composed. And he waited.

"Hi, yourself." She extended her hand, reaching out for him.

His fingers wound tightly around hers and she led him into the room and shut the door. When she turned back to face him, he held her silk scarf in his hand.

So perhaps he was here in response to her invitation after all. She reminded herself to take things light and easy. And she would have laughed at her foolish longings if not for the pain twisting and strangling her heart.

Mallory forcibly shrugged it off. Once she was away from this plush resort and Jack's compelling intensity, she'd immerse herself in work and put this interlude behind her. But in the meantime, if she was going to have the fantasies she might as well indulge them.

She stepped backward into the room. Jack followed until her knees hit the bed and she fell onto her back. She licked at her dry lips. "Did you make out okay at home?"

His gaze dropped to the rise and fall of her chest, the swell of her breasts visible above one of the silk teddies she favored for sleeping.

His pupils dilated with obvious desire. "We can talk about it later." It wasn't a suggestion.

He loomed over her, large and feral, masculine and demanding and she had no wish to deny him anything he wanted. His hands bracketed her head and his lower body cradled hers, pushing her into the mattress. The hard ridge of his erection thrusting through heavy denim nestled between her legs, against the soft silk barrier of her panties.

He stretched her arms out over her head, the scarf still held in one hand. "What did you plan on doing with this?"

She treated him to a sexy grin. "We can talk about it later." She shimmied her hips upward in blatant invitation.

"How is it you know exactly what I need?" Another question he obviously didn't want answered because before she could respond, he covered her mouth with his.

His lips were hot, his hands even hotter as he kissed her for all he was worth and explored her body, leaving a branding sensation wherever he touched. Little finesse was involved as he grabbed for the strap on her teddy and pulled it off her shoulders, following a scorching path with his lips and tongue.

All the while she fumbled, trying to free her hands from his grasp so she could reach for the snap on his pants but he held on tight, obviously needing to control and dominate. And though she'd spent most of her career trying *not* to be submissive to any man, this was personal.

This was Jack and she didn't mind yielding right now. Not when what awaited her was certain to be worth it.

He released her arms and slid down her body until his lips reached her breasts. He latched on to one nipple through the lacy silk covering, pulling the rigid peak into his mouth. Soft suckling alternated with teasing flickers of his tongue and ended with a soft scraping of his teeth against her sensitive flesh.

She let out a cry of surprise as sensation traveled a direct path from her breast to the moist place between her thighs—the place she needed him most, but he hadn't chosen that route.

Yet.

Instead he soothed the places he'd nipped with erotic laps of his tongue that were so exquisitely painful she saw white starbursts behind her closed eyelids.

"Better?" he asked.

"Mmm." Speaking was beyond her. Her body was on fire, an empty, aching raging inferno of need.

He levered himself up on his elbows and met her gaze. "I should slow down." But from the heat in his eyes and the dark flush on his cheeks, slow was the last thing he wanted.

"Not for my sake I hope." She let out a strangled laugh. "Any slower and I might die first."

"Me, too." He brushed her dark hair off her flushed cheek. "So far be it for me to deny you."

13

JACK LOOKED at her face. No, he couldn't deny her. Especially when he needed her so badly. He hadn't realized how much until he'd looked into her compassionate, blue eyes.

He glanced down. Her breasts rose and fell beneath the nearly sheer lingerie and having tasted the sweetness beneath, Jack desired more.

And obviously so did she. He pulled hard on the thin strap on her shoulder and it tore from its binding. He did the same to the other strap and eased the teddy off her, as she lifted her back and hips, all too eager to shed the constricting undergarments.

What he saw was beyond his wildest imaginings. If he'd walked into this room at the boiling point, looking at her naked body shattered what remained of both his reserve and his restraint. "You're incredible."

She averted her gaze. "Can we stick to the truth?"

"Absolutely." She obviously still didn't believe in her beauty or worth and given what he'd learned of her history he understood.

But when she was with him, dammit, she shouldn't have to doubt. He drew back and stood, stripping quickly, divesting himself of his clothes until he could join her again on the bed. Heat arced between them, hot and powerful.

Her eyes bore into him, watching his erection. "You see what you do to me." She was seeing him naked yes, but she also saw inside him, deeper than any woman had before.

A wry, yet adorable smile twisted her lips. "It's a known fact men don't always think with their...well you know, when they're looking to get lucky."

He laughed at her forthright response. That was *his* Mallory, the honest woman who didn't hold back what she was thinking. "I wouldn't call it *getting lucky* if it was just an easy lay with someone I didn't give a damn about."

Her lashes fluttered, showing her uncertainty. "Well it's also a known fact men will say many things in the heat of the moment and mean very few of them."

"We're not in the heat of the moment." He eased forward until he could push her legs apart and kneel between. "Yet." He kept his gaze on hers but bent lower, his lips inches from paradise.

She let out a slow exhale of air. "You talk a good game." And her husky voice told him how much she liked his talk—as well as his obvious intent.

"It's no game. If all I wanted was any woman, I wouldn't be here now." Because she was too damn complicated, too compelling, too everything as far as he was concerned.

If he lost himself inside her to forget the pain of the day, he risked losing himself to her forever. But he was here and too far gone. He wasn't running away.

"And sweetheart, if all I wanted was any woman, I'd be inside you by now, taking care of my needs instead of doing this." He dipped his head and licked her, tasting her femininity, feeling her heat and fueling the dewy dampness.

"Believe me now?" he asked.

A shuddering moan was her only response. Her hands gripped the bedding by his side and her hips jerked upward. From her liquid heat Jack knew she was close to the edge and he couldn't wait any longer. Good thing he didn't have to worry about readying her for the next step.

She caught him off guard, toppling him over onto his back, straddling his waist. He barely saw her reach for the drawer or rip open the foil packet, but he most definitely felt her ease the moist plastic sheath over his penis, and pause for deliberate handling that went above and beyond merely donning protection.

The desire to drive himself inside her was strong. The need to watch her as she lowered herself onto him and accommodated his width and length even stronger. But he couldn't stop himself from touching her, from taking his fingertips and parting her feminine flesh and from placing himself at her opening.

He grabbed for her hips at the same moment she released her restraint. He slid inside her heated core, feeling her slick and moist passage close around him.

"God." The word erupted from him in a guttural groan. Her body's initial resistance was his tight consummate pleasure. He'd never felt anything so hot, so right, so *perfect,* he thought, and their fit brought a choking sensation to his throat.

And because he'd promised himself he'd watch, he forced his heavy eyelids open and pushing himself up on his elbows, he glanced down. Big mistake, he thought as he viewed himself cushioned inside her body. If he thought he'd be a goner before he knew he was lost now.

Or was he actually found? Shaking off the intense thoughts in favor of intense pleasure he began a steady thrusting motion that intensified every sensation rocketing through his body.

Mallory nearly screamed from the incredible heat and dizzying friction they were creating. She was wet silk surrounding hardened flesh. Though she thought she'd steeled herself against an overload of emotion, she'd been wrong.

What she felt for this man was so powerful and strong, it would remain with her long after *they* were no more, something she didn't want to think about yet. She clenched her muscles tighter around his hard, straining erection, knowing her climax was in sight.

Her grinding met with his thrusting resistance and the tantalizing waves grew stronger. Jack grabbed on to her hips and she opened her eyes to meet his clouded but steady gaze. "Let yourself go, sweetheart." He lifted his hips, bringing her so close. And he waited.

She tried to breathe and a needy cry came out instead. "Then you take me there—and come with me." She swiveled her bottom in a slow circular motion. Her pelvis gyrated into his hips and he penetrated so deep the word joining took on a whole new meaning.

"Aah, God. Now." He thrust and she tightened her muscles around him.

Swirling waves of unending pleasure swamped her. She looked into his incredible face and meeting her gaze, he pumped harder. She couldn't think let alone breathe. Their bodies moved together in unison, his thrusting movements coming faster and faster until her grinding resistance became the focal point of erotic pleasure.

"Yes, yes..." She let out a cry of pleasure in a voice she didn't recognize as her own.

"Yes." He echoed her words as he came, bursting inside her as he shook with the power of his orgasm.

And the world as she knew it fragmented into millions of pieces of light, blindsiding her—not by the release itself, but because this time they came together—and the beauty brought tears to her eyes.

Her breathing came in shallow gasps as she dropped her body weight onto his. "I love you." The words escaped before she could stop them and considering what had come before, she couldn't call them back even if she wanted to.

She didn't. And that scared her most of all.

MALLORY LAY on top of him, breathless, sated...and expecting an answer, if Jack's hunch was right. But he had nothing to say. Nothing she'd want to hear, anyway.

Before Mallory, Jack had always had sex. He'd had a damn good hunch as he walked into this room, that *this* was much more. He'd been right. She wasn't the only one falling.

Years of preconceived notions and divorce statistics told him they didn't stand a chance, yet for the first time he considered the other statistics. The marriages that survived. The people who stayed together for reasons that transcended convenience and security. He was willing to look the idea of a soul mate in the eye and not run for protection.

He didn't miss the irony. The one time in his life he was willing to face the future, he didn't have one.

Mallory exhaled and he felt the whoosh of air against his cheek. "I won't lie and say I said it in the heat of the moment, but don't worry, I don't expect you to say *I love you* back."

"I do care." More than was prudent. "And I wish I could say the words." But he couldn't acknowledge he might feel the same because to do so would jeopardize everything she wanted out of life.

Jack was the least selfless person he knew, yet protecting Mallory and the things she held dear had become his priority. Her career most of all.

"Hey, wishing doesn't make things happen and we both knew the rules going in."

Jack didn't buy her lighthearted tone. "Rules change."

"But outlooks don't. And we both know yours."

He forced a laugh he didn't feel. "Yes, it parallels yours. Career first. Everything else second."

"Right."

Yet suddenly faced with the thought of returning

to his empty New York City apartment didn't feel as invigorating or liberating as it once had.

But he'd already made partner, already achieved his dream. Whatever her reasons for wanting to make partner, and regardless of whether it would alter her relationship with her parents, that was her goal. One she'd worked and strived for. One she'd suppressed her sense of self to achieve.

I love you.

He couldn't admit he felt the same. Couldn't confront his own demons and decide whether to take the risk and trust Mallory with his heart. He had no choice but to push the truth away.

For her sake.

From violating the no-office-romance policy to playing around on the job, the old guard at the firm would view Mallory's actions with disdain. They wouldn't fire Mallory—they couldn't without risk of a lawsuit—but they could stall her partnership and make her miserable until she left on her own. They wouldn't mourn the loss of their only female associate. Meanwhile Jack would get a reprimand, a slap on the hand and maybe even a ribald joke about controlling his baser urges. But he'd have his partnership and his career intact. Unfair, but true.

''Jack?''

He rolled to the side, taking her with him. Her flesh pressed against his, warming him. He glanced into her worried face and admitted to himself he cared about her too damn much. ''I'm here.''

But he didn't love her, Mallory thought. Her heart twisted with regret. Even if fate dictated they had no future, she wished he felt the same. But she figured he was too used to the line to take her seriously anyway. No matter how much her pounding heart already belonged to him.

"What happened at home?" she asked, changing the subject.

He visibly winced. "My parents are getting divorced, finally."

"So your father stood up for himself. You must be pleased."

"Pleased doesn't begin to describe it. My mother went home to pack her things—boyfriend by her side."

Mallory cringed. "That's insensitive."

His expression turned shuttered and blank. "That's my mother."

And that's where Jack's views on long-term relationships and women came from, Mallory realized.

"Onward and upward. She constantly wants more and better and doesn't care who gets hurt on her way."

"Why did she stay with him so long then?" she asked of Jack's father.

"Financial security. And he allowed it."

"We're not all like her." Mallory wasn't sure where the words came from, only that they were necessary.

"I know you aren't." A muscle ticked in his clenched jaw. "But forgive me for not having tested the theory. The divorces and statistics I've seen were enough to convince me to steer clear."

She shut her mouth and nodded. Perhaps he believed she was different, perhaps not. In the end it didn't matter because he'd bought into a stereotype too difficult for any woman to overcome. Especially Mallory, who'd made her climb up the ladder, *her onward and upward,* a public one in a male dominated world.

She placed a hand over his lips. He'd already confided enough to convince her he trusted her with his personal, emotional baggage. She wouldn't make him dredge up more. "I can think of more fun things to do than get all emotional."

His dark eyes met hers, and in those depths she saw a wealth of emotion and feeling—and she refused to believe she'd conjured it up in her mind. That he'd fallen for her a little bit was enough considering they each had their own paths to follow, neither allowing for a long-term relationship.

"What'd you have in mind?" he asked.

She forced an easy smile. "I heard from our P.I. and I have a wealth of information about Mrs. Lederman." But laying naked with Jack, for what might be the last time, she had no wish to discuss work. Especially a topic which pained her more each time she thought about it.

His big hand cupped her hip. "You didn't have work in mind."

She shook her head. "And it's not like there's anything we can do with the information at midnight."

"You're right. Whatever it is can wait." He covered her mouth with his and drew her into a deep kiss. And when he bit down on her lower lip, she moaned.

She desired more but knew she had other things in store for Jack and forced herself to pull back. She grabbed for the scarf he'd brought with him that lay beside her on the bed, then she rose to a sitting position, settling herself above his stomach.

She wrapped the scarf around her hands and pulled at the opposite ends, teasingly. Enticingly.

His eyes darkened with anticipation. "Exactly what do you plan on doing with that thing?"

"I thought I'd have my wicked way with you again. You see I've heard that if you blindfold a man, his other senses become that much more acute."

"Interesting theory," he said.

She grinned. "I thought so. Do you think the same holds true for women?"

"I certainly intend to find out." He pushed his upper body forward so he could raise himself off the mattress and nip at one nipple, causing waves of pleasure to crest and recede inside her. She bent her head back and let out a muffled cry.

While she was distracted, he grabbed the scarf from her hands. "Cheater." She barely got the words out when he pulled the fabric taut to rub it in a horizontal motion across her breasts. Her hips began an involuntary circular dance on his stomach.

"I don't see you complaining," he said with a grin.

Light and fun. He'd relaxed once more. At least she hadn't scared him away with her declaration of love. She supposed not asking for anything in return helped him push her declaration out of his mind, and if she were smart, she'd do the same herself.

He wound his hands around the silk, his heavy lidded gaze never leaving hers. "Let's test those heightened senses of yours."

She sucked in a nervous breath. She'd planned on pleasuring him this way, not having the tables turned. Her nipples had already hardened into tight peaks and the dewy moisture between her legs attested to her growing excitement. As he secured the scarf around her eyes, everything around her went black.

Anticipation coiled into a knot in her stomach. The nerve endings in her fingertips began to tingle and as suggested, her other senses grew stronger.

She inhaled. The scent of his cologne, potent and alluring teased her already tenuous restraint while goose bumps arose on her arms thanks to the air-conditioning in the room—and the inherent foreplay in his actions.

A cool rush of air blew over her nipples. She arched her back at the sensual assault and would have fallen over if not for Jack's strong arm around her waist.

"I've got you." He eased her backward onto the fluffy mound of pillows behind her.

Curiosity hammered a rapid beat in her veins. She was vulnerable to him and his intentions, yet she'd never trusted a man more. "Jack?"

"Right here." He brushed a soft kiss over her lips, then adjusted her blindfold, making certain she couldn't see but allowing for comfort. Seconds later, soft music floated around the room. "Are you okay?" he asked.

"Never better." She heard the warmth infused into

her voice, and knew it was a reflection of how he made her feel.

"Good. Now let's test that theory of yours."

"There are five senses, yes?"

She nodded.

Jack intended to test every one. He couldn't give her more than now, but when now was over, she'd have not only her love but a host of memories to hold on to and he'd have the same.

So why didn't it seem enough?

He shivered, knowing what he really wanted was to lose himself inside her once more and this time, he'd be the one to let go of his tightly reined emotions. Restrained by reality, he had no choice but to give back the only other way he could—in return for the love she'd offered him and he'd had to turn away.

"So which of those five senses do you want to start with first?" he asked.

Her lips turned upward in a grin. "I think that would have to be touch."

He nearly broke into a sweat just thinking about all the ways he wanted to explore her body and let her *feel* him.

He grit his teeth. Not yet. "Sorry but we're saving the best for last. Let's go with taste. Sit tight."

"Like I'm going anywhere?" she asked wryly.

He headed for the minibar beneath the television. Thank goodness for amenities because in the refrigerator, he found a bar of chocolate. After unwrapping the candy, he took a bite of the milk chocolate and caramel and chewed. And chewed. And chewed.

"Hey what's going on there?" she asked into the silence.

He laughed, realizing how long it was taking him to break down and finish the luscious treat. "Not a thing. You ready?"

"I've been ready." She followed the statement with a long groan that he swallowed with his mouth as he covered her lips with his.

Mallory caught on quick. Her tongue invaded his mouth and began a long and leisurely exploration. She lapped at his tongue and nibbled on his bottom lip before coming up for air. "Mmm. Delicious."

The husky sound shook him to his core and if he'd been sated minutes before, he was aroused again now.

"Chocolate."

"Very good. Ready for the next one?"

She licked her moist lips. The erotic gesture sent shooting darts of desire straight to his groin.

Somehow he managed to suck in a breath and hold off tossing her onto the mattress. They had an experiment to complete first.

"Sense of smell, okay?" He turned her to face him, placing her hands on his shoulders.

After his shower and before leaving for the city, he'd splashed aftershave on and headed out the door. If his scent worked on her the way her exotic, unique scent worked on him, he'd have to pull her off him after this test.

He grabbed her hips and said, "Scoot forward and wrap your legs around my waist."

A few misses and some jockeying of positions later, she'd done as he requested. Her thighs bracketed his waist and her damp, feminine heat pressed warm and enticingly against his groin.

"What are you doing to me?" Her words came out more of a whimper than a question.

Jack understood. His body was strung tight and begged for completion. But just being cocooned against Mallory and knowing it would have to last him a lifetime enabled him to savor the experience. And wait.

He kissed her lips. "Arousing you, sweetheart. Just like you'd intended to do to me with this scarf of yours."

She scrunched up her nose. "I'll have to pay you back, you know."

He laughed hard. "I'm shaking. Now rest your head right here." He guided her chin onto his shoulder.

She nuzzled her soft cheek against his roughened one and they sat in silence as her heart beat fast and strong against his chest. Her breasts softened against him and the head of his penis nudged against her opening, unprotected and insistent.

He prayed for restraint.

"You're breathing fast," she noted, a playful teasing tone in her voice. "Hard and shallow. Does that count for my heightened sense of hearing?"

If it brought him closer to the end of this experiment, hell yes, Jack thought. "It's fine."

She snuggled cheek to cheek for a moment before burying her face between his neck and shoulder. Her skin was soft, her breathing as shallow as his. She lifted her arms around his waist, hugging him close.

That fast the gesture became more intimate than experimental. More an honest expression of emotion than a light and easy game.

Jack clung to the remaining strength he had left. Until she began to nuzzle his neck with her nose.

"Musky," she murmured. "Masculine." The words vibrated near his ear. "And so sexy." She nipped the skin on his neck with her teeth then soothed with her tongue.

He'd ached. Now his body shook and restraint became a memory. The experimenting was over. It'd been harder on him than on her anyway. He'd survived taste, smell and hearing. Now he wanted touch.

Drawing her down to the bed he pulled the scarf off her eyes. She blinked as she adjusted to the light.

He looked into her face. "I want touch."

Her lips parted. "Me, too. God, me, too." Her permission was all he needed. He nudged her legs wide and drove himself into her.

He drove himself home.

MALLORY PULLED herself to a sitting position and watched Jack sleep. His tanned chest rose and fell and the warmth emanating from him drew her toward him all over again. She lay back and curled into him. His arms immediately reached out and cradled her in comfort and security. Desire hovered beneath the surface, a secondary emotion to her love for this man.

With this relationship she'd violated Mallory Sinclair, Esq.'s ethics and aspirations yet she couldn't regret discovering Mallory Sinclair, the woman, and revealing her buried emotions. And though Jack said he couldn't return her feelings and wouldn't want a relationship that extended beyond this trip, Mallory would walk away from this experience forever changed.

For the first time in her life, she realized *her* feelings and needs came before her desire to please her father, a man who'd never shown any interest in her life or career. So why had she planned her entire future around attempting to gain his respect and love?

No answer came. But with dawn breaking outside her window, she realized the career path she'd chosen for the wrong reasons conflicted with acting upon the private investigator's revelations regarding Mrs. Lederman.

And it was past time she dealt with certain facts and faced up to her feelings.

"Are you up?" Jack's morning-roughened voice sounded in her ear.

"Mmm. I've been thinking."

"About last night, I hope." His hand reached around to cup her breast.

The pleasing tingling started immediately but her mind was worked up and she needed to talk first. "Last night was amazing. But we need to talk work before we get sidetracked again."

He laughed. "You want me to talk work while I'm in bed with you and more awake with each passing minute?" He inched closer, until his groin, hard and erect, nestled against her back.

She let out a sigh. "Hard as it is..."

When he chuckled, she caught his double meaning

and laughed. "No, hard as it is for me to say no to you now, I need to get this information off my chest."

"What is it?" he asked, sounding concerned.

"Alicia Lederman has a history of abusing prescription drugs."

"Bingo!"

Mallory cringed at the excitement she heard in his voice.

"This is exactly what we need to force her into a settlement. Once we tell Lederman about this... Wait a damn minute." Behind her, Jack pulled himself to a sitting position.

Not wanting to feel exposed, she yanked the covers over her chest and sat up, too. "What's wrong?"

"Was this abuse while they were married?"

Mallory nodded. "So was her stay in an expensive rehab clinic."

"Then why didn't Lederman share this piece of information?"

"Well we're not his attorneys of record," she reminded him.

"I can buy that. But there's another possibility—"

"He was testing us," Mallory said, finishing his thought and sharing her own conclusions at the same time. "He wanted to see if we'd uncover the information on our own and how far we were willing to go with it." And Mallory wasn't willing to go the distance on this one.

She wasn't sure when she'd made the decision, but it was somewhere between getting to know and like Alicia Lederman and falling in love with Jack. A soft side she hadn't realized existed had crept up on her and settled in.

Mallory couldn't use the woman's past against her. Even if it cost her her job and the partnership she'd thought she'd coveted. She admired and respected Alicia Lederman too much. Her sense of fairness dictated she take the woman's feelings into account.

Without warning, Jack tossed off the covers and climbed out of bed.

"Where are you going?"

"To talk to that son of a bitch. It's one thing to be undecided about counsel and to invite us out here to get to know us better, but it's another to play the games he's been playing, disappearing, withholding information. I'm through. Either my record speaks for itself or it doesn't." He grabbed for his jeans.

"Jack, wait."

He paused. "You're right. I'll shower first and then I'll tackle Paul Lederman." He charged toward the bathroom, magnificent in his nudity and masculinity.

She licked at her dry lips. "What's the plan, Jack?"

He paused and turned. "Before or after I strangle him?" he asked wryly.

"After."

"He hires us and we use the information and agree to as small a settlement as possible, why?"

"Because I vote we don't use it."

Jack stalked back into the room, his attorney instincts kicking into gear. "Mind telling me why not?"

She shook her head. "Because she doesn't deserve it. You heard her. She raised his kids and from what

I've seen she's a major player in running this place. She's earned a fair share. Besides, if she had a drug problem, she's obviously over it now. Why threaten to make her weakness public? Why set her kids up for ridicule just to achieve Mr. Lederman's needs?''

''Because if he comes around like I expect him to, he'll be our client.'' A client Jack didn't like and didn't trust, but a client entitled to loyalty and the best representation for his money just the same.

He stood at the foot of the bed, recalling their first day at the resort, Mallory's determination and no-holds-bar attitude toward getting to know Mrs. Lederman and aiding their client.

''*You* suggested hiring the private investigator in the first place. Now you want to bury the information you asked him to find?'' Jack shook his head in disbelief. ''Aside from the fact that I doubt Lederman will want that, it's contrary to our legal ethics and what we owe the client.''

She narrowed her gaze, obviously furious that he'd questioned her ethics. ''I just happen to think there are less slimy tactics available.'' But she glanced away just as quickly, a sure sign more was going on inside that beautiful head than she was willing to let on.

''This from the woman who wants to make it in a man's world?'' He could have bitten his tongue in two the minute the words escaped his mouth. But she'd shocked him with her about-face.

His arguments *for* using the information were valid. And besides, if he wanted things between them to return to a normal professional level, he couldn't tread lightly around her feelings just because they'd once been involved.

Were still involved. *Dammit*. He didn't like this one bit.

She rose from the bed, wrapping the sheet around her in what seemed more like an emotionally protective gesture than a physical one. "Well I guess we know where we both stand on this issue. And whose opinion carries the most weight."

He hated hurting her. He hated the distance he'd just put between them even more. "Mallory..."

She shook her head. "Go shower and talk to Lederman."

Knowing there was nothing more to say, Jack pulled on his pants and retreated to his own room for a shower. By the time he'd cooled down and knocked on her door, no one answered.

Whether she'd headed downstairs for a walk on the beach or if she was just ignoring him, the result was the same.

He was alone.

14

JACK STRODE into the crowded gym. Seven-thirty in the morning was prime workout time when the sun beckoned for the rest of the day. Looking around, he spotted his mark standing by the treadmill, white towel wrapped around his beefy neck.

Jack steeled himself for the argument to come. He'd been too damn lax on this trip. Too distracted by the thrill of the game he and Mallory had played.

He walked over to the corner of the room. "Paul. I'd like a word with you." Jack refrained from showing his anger or frustration yet. There was still a remote chance his gut instinct regarding Lederman's motives were wrong. But he doubted it.

Lederman turned—reluctantly—away from the treadmill and met Jack's stare. "I was going to give you a call this afternoon."

Sure he was. Since his return, he'd been making himself scarce. And because of Jack's affair with Mallory, he'd been too preoccupied to care. But if her chilly attitude this morning was any indication, the honeymoon was over, and maybe it was for the best.

"What's up?" Paul asked.

"Why don't you tell me. I've spent four days here and not a word from you. Meanwhile my sources tell me you've been holding out on me." Jack glanced around to make sure no one was in hearing distance. "Prescription drug abuse?" Jack watched Lederman's reaction closely.

"How the hell did you come up with that?" Paul narrowed his gaze, then shrugged. "No matter now. It's ripe for use." He narrowed his gaze. "You willing to use it?"

"*If* you hire me, and *if* that's what you want and *if* it makes strategic sense, then yes." As he spoke, the look of disappointment in Mallory's face flashed before his eyes and his stomach knotted in self-disgust.

His father's pleading face came next. Jack didn't have to question how he would react if his parents' divorce got messy and his greedy mother decided to use his father's weaknesses and shortcomings against him. Nor did he question the names he'd be calling the lawyer who was willing to represent his mother and play those dirty games. Games Jack had been playing for years with other people's divorces and unspared feelings.

Lederman let out a loud laugh. "I've done some digging of my own. You've got yourself a damn good record, obviously a damn good team of investigators *and* you've got balls. I like that in a man." Without warning, Paul held out his hand. "Consider yourself hired."

Jack forced himself to shake Lederman's hand. "You won't be sorry. Waldorf, Haynes will give you the best representation out there. But there's one thing we need to settle first."

"What's that?"

Jack stepped into Lederman's personal space. "I might be willing to play hardball, but I don't appreciate having it played against me by my own client. My reputation precedes me," Jack said, not caring how arrogant he sounded. "Either you trust my ability or you don't. Next time you play games I'm out of here."

"Deal." Lederman pumped his hand with enthusiasm before excusing himself and turning back to the treadmill that awaited him.

Jack walked back through the gym. He'd just accomplished a huge coup. He'd secured his firm's largest client and kept the eccentric man happy at the same time. And though Lederman was slime, Jack hadn't agreed to dirty his hands or compromise his professional work ethic.

He hadn't agreed to go any further on this client's behalf than he'd done many times before. But instead of feeling ecstatic, instead of the usual rush of adrenaline he'd experienced in the past, Jack's stomach twisted into tight knots. Because despite the positive outcome of the business side of this trip, he had the uneasy feeling this case would reverberate through his life in unexpected ways—jeopardizing the future he'd never thought he wanted.

The one he'd never have.

Though he wasn't looking forward to the confrontation, Jack owed Mallory an update regarding his conversation with Lederman. And with their return to the office imminent, they needed a frank discussion about what had gone on between them as well.

Not to mention that Jack *needed* one last time alone with Mallory before reality set in.

MALLORY ZIPPED her suitcase closed. She had to get out of here and back to her life before she lost her sense of self. Falling in love with Jack, she'd discovered one Mallory and lost another. The one that was goal-oriented and on the fast track to partnership. The one who never thought she wanted a husband or family. The one content to hide her femininity.

The one who considered Jack an unattainable dream.

She could never put the new Mallory behind her any more than she could completely return to the ice princess who'd been Waldorf, Haynes's top associate. The feminine, erotic woman was a part of her now. So, too, was the woman who considered Alicia Lederman's feelings more important than making partner.

She'd changed. There would have to be more changes when she got home. Spending more time with Jack Latham would never allow her to get over the one and probably only love of her life. The one who distrusted women, relationships and love. The one who'd come to her on a dare and continued on only because each challenge became harder to resist.

The one who didn't believe in dreams or happily ever after.

The ringing of the telephone startled her out of her deep thoughts. She picked up the receiver. "Hello?"

"Ms. Sinclair?" A deep male voice she didn't recognize answered her.

"Yes. Who is this please?"

"The hotel concierge. I've been asked to inform you to meet your business partner in room 520 at eight o'clock this evening."

Jack's room across the hall. Her heart began a rapid, thudding beat. A keen sense of longing took hold, the emotions strong and overwhelming. "Thank you," she murmured into the phone.

A lump that might as well have been Mallory's heart lodged in her throat. Not an invitation but a business meeting. And certainly not a returned declaration of love.

Mallory Sinclair, Esq. would never deny a partner's request. But Mallory Sinclair, woman, had no choice. She was smart enough to know when to give in. She lifted her suitcase onto the floor.

There was no way she could handle one last meeting with Jack. Not with her heart in shreds and her career at a crossroad.

She didn't fault Jack for his attitude this morning. Using the private investigator's report was the right move—for someone who wanted to represent Paul Lederman. She didn't need to forgive Jack for doing his job. It was the same strategic move she would have made the day she'd arrived at the resort. But no longer.

Along with finding herself came a clarity and acceptance of life she hadn't had before. The same way she knew she'd never change her parents' lack of feeling for their only child, she now knew she couldn't change Jack's negative views on love and relationships. Lord knows she'd tried.

Too bad she'd been the only one to undergo self-revelation on this trip or she wouldn't have to leave the resort alone. She and Jack could go—together.

She wiped at the tear dripping down her cheek. She'd begun this game with an invitation aimed at teaching him a lesson. He'd returned the favor and they'd engaged in a sensual, exciting competition, each trying to top the other—neither realizing one of them would end up with a broken heart. Until it was too late.

So no, she wouldn't show up, not even for a business meeting. She'd find a way to get the message to him so she didn't stand him up. And then she'd head home.

Alone.

JACK PACED the floor of his room. At nine o'clock he realized Mallory wasn't going to show. At ten o'clock, one stiff drink later and well into seventh inning stretch of the Yankees game, there was a knock at the door.

Professionally he should have been furious she was so late, but at this point his heart was thinking for him and his emotions were keyed. He was angry and hurt as hell. Be it a business summons or a personal request, the very least she could have done was send him a polite "no thank you."

His head was pounding and his throat raw. He felt like crap and realized Mallory was just a part of it. All he needed on top of things was the damn flu. He rose from the couch and walked to the door. On the other side was Alicia Lederman—the last person Jack expected to see.

"Can I help you?"

"I've got a message for you." The older woman held out a white envelope with the resort logo on the upper lefthand corner. "I promised to bring this over earlier. Much earlier. But we had an emergency in the lobby. A man had a heart attack and I had to call the hotel doctor and 9-1-1..." She shook her head. "Anyway, here it is with my sincere apologies."

"No need to apologize." Considering what Jack had in store for her, *he* ought to be saying "I'm sorry."

The thought jarred him, taking him by surprise. When had he ever felt the need to apologize for doing his job? He glanced at Alicia. Though she looked as elegant as ever, the weariness in her face tugged at Jack's heart. He wondered if he was truly seeing her for the first time or viewing her through Mallory's eyes. Either way he didn't like what he saw and wondered if Mallory was right—if there was a way of settling this divorce without causing needless pain and heartache.

He met Alicia's gaze, impressed with her dignity and courage. "You could have sent a bellboy with this." He waved the note in the air. "Why bring it yourself?"

"Because if Mallory cares, then you must be a good man in here." She tapped the area near her heart.

He wouldn't touch that assumption. "You've spoken with her then."

Alicia nodded. "Before she left. She's on her way home. I'm sure that note explains it all."

He stepped back. "Come in, please."

Alicia followed him inside but remained silent, obviously sensing he needed space. And he did. So Mallory hadn't stood him up—not in the way he'd thought anyway. But the truth didn't make him feel any better and his stomach churned with remorse.

Jack didn't care if he had an audience, he just wanted to know what Mallory had to say. He pulled the scented paper from the envelope and read silently.

While I regret not telling you in person, I'm smart enough not to engage in a battle I can't win.

This trip taught me a lot about myself and what I want out of life.

I'm going home to begin making some changes. And regretfully I'm going to have to let this last meeting pass.

It was fun while it lasted.

Love,
Mallory

The pain in Jack's gut grew larger.

"Endings are never easy." Alicia placed a hand on his arm, then embarrassed, she withdrew quickly.

Jack met her sympathetic gaze. "I guess you would know," he said, careful to let kindness not sarcasm infuse his voice.

She nodded. "I realize I can't keep Paul if he doesn't want to stay. And I know you thought I was ignoring you when you told me to get an attorney, but I wasn't. I was preparing."

"And keeping your cards close to your vest. I respect that."

"I'm not certain what I've done deserves it. But what I do know is that the marriage is over. And I refuse to go without a fight."

"You realize this is when I advise you to get counsel." She was so easy to talk to, Jack couldn't help but smile.

"I will. But I was hoping we could deal first." Reaching into her bag, she held out a manila envelope. "I'm not as naive as my husband thinks. There's some information on me that I am certain he'll want to use. Let him know I've got ammunition of my own."

Jack quickly thumbed through the contents of the package—incriminating photos of Paul Lederman and a young woman. Dates noting the ongoing relationship were clear on each photo. Alicia Lederman had proof of her husband's infidelity. Jack let out a groan.

"She's an employee," Alicia said. "A very young, inexperienced employee." The hurt in her voice was unmistakable. "I swear to you he wasn't like this when we married. The heart attack and middle age changed him." She shook her head, disgust etched in her features.

Jack could empathize. Paul Lederman's actions made him sick. "Are you planning to use these?"

The older woman wiped at her eyes. "I don't want them made public, no. I've got children who are more important than any money I get out of the divorce settlement."

Jack stood before Alicia Lederman, at a loss for

words. Here was a woman with proof in her hands, proof that could net her a huge settlement if she pushed hard enough, but she was willing to put aside the cash for the sake of her children. She was so different than any client or spouse he'd ever encountered.

She was unique. And so was Mallory who'd seen this woman's goodness from day one.

"Mr. Latham?"

He cleared his throat. "Sorry. If you're not willing to use these why are you showing them to me?"

"I said I don't want them made public, not that I wouldn't use them if forced."

Through her pain, Jack heard the determination in her voice and respected her for it.

"Make no mistake. I'd take my licking if Paul insisted on using the information on me, and I don't want to drag my children through the mud twice. They need to believe they've got one parent they can look up to. Even if it's a charade. So you show him these—they're copies by the way—and tell him all I want is what's fair. I've helped run this resort and raised his kids. I'm middle-aged with no other source of income or abilities. All I'm asking for is a fair and equitable settlement so he can't squander it on those young women he prefers."

She choked back a sob and Jack felt the lump rise in his throat. Not only for Alicia but for his own father who was going through the same ordeal.

"I'm hoping the threat of these photos is enough. But if he backs me into a corner, I'll come out fighting."

"I understand." Jack stood with the envelope in his hand, knowing his firm's largest client had sealed his own fate.

Jack hesitated, then put a hand on Alicia's shoulder. "I'll show him and advise him accordingly. In the meantime, you get yourself a lawyer first thing tomorrow."

She nodded, gratitude flickering in her eyes. "Mallory was right about you. You just need to realize it on your own. Goodbye, Mr. Latham."

"Good night."

Alicia slipped out the door, leaving Jack alone with the incriminating photos and Mallory's note. He walked over to the large mirror in the master bedroom. He braced his hands on the counter and looked into the reflective glass. He barely recognized the man facing him. He'd never considered himself a coward, yet that's exactly what he was looking at. A man who, like his father, was afraid to take the step that would forever change his life.

Although both he and Mallory had known the rules going into the affair, neither had followed those rules. She'd fallen in love and had the courage to admit the truth. He'd fallen, too, but when faced with her admission he'd hidden behind the excuse of protecting her—instead of facing up to his greatest fear and overcoming it.

The irony was clear. Jack was a man who'd spent his life running from love and commitment until he'd walked right into its trap.

Only loving Mallory didn't feel like a trap. The rest of his so-called life did.

"You *what?*"

Mallory dumped the box of her personal things on the floor of the apartment she shared with her cousin. "I quit, Julia. *Q-U-I-T.* What don't you understand?"

Actually she'd given two weeks' notice, but the senior partner wasn't interested in keeping her on. Not after he'd heard she wasn't willing to use the information against Alicia Lederman. Jack had been out with the flu since they got back and the Lederman case had fallen into Mallory's hands. She'd chosen to walk before setting Alicia Lederman up for pain and heartache.

Upon Mallory's departure from the resort, she'd bid Alicia an emotional goodbye. Because of her professional ethics, which at this point she wanted to choke on, Mallory hadn't been able to do more than advise the other woman to get an attorney. But she refused to be the one to feed Alicia to her husband, the shark.

"Come sit down." Julia patted the seat on the couch. "By the time I got home last night you were fast asleep and the first time I see you today, you've quit a job you'd dedicated your life to. You were this close to making partner." She pinched her thumb and forefinger together and her silver bracelets jangled against each other. "So what gives?"

Mallory eyed her cousin warily as she settled in beside her. "You've got dark circles under your eyes and you've been suspiciously silent and you're asking *me* what gives?"

Julia rolled her eyes. "I'm not the one who spent

five days at a resort with the firm's most eligible partner.''

Mallory hugged her shoulders tight. ''He's not eligible.'' And as of the end of her first week back, he hadn't returned to the office, either. So she'd avoided any awkward confrontation and by having her notice declined, she'd probably avoided ever seeing him again. That damned lump in her throat returned.

''Not eligible? You mean he was engaged or married during *that one night?* What a slime.'' Julia made a face accompanied by a snort of disgust.

Despite herself, Mallory chuckled. She had no intention of revealing to Julia it had been much more than one night. ''He's neither engaged nor married but he's just as unavailable in here.'' She tapped her chest, above her heart. ''And here.'' She gestured towards her head.

And if all their intimate time together hadn't changed his outlook nothing would.

Julia leaned forward to give Mallory a comforting embrace and she was grateful for her cousin's silent, solid support.

Julia pulled back. ''Did he say for certain he's not interested or are you guessing? Because even the most determined bachelor can meet his match.'' A wicked gleam lit Julia's gaze.

''Don't tell me you believe in the right woman changing a stubborn man's mind.''

''I'm just saying not to give up hope until you've heard it from the horse's mouth.'' Julia grinned. ''So to speak.''

''I don't think he has anything more to say to me.

Once you tell someone you love them, the ball pretty much falls into their court.''

She sighed. "I can't argue that though I wish I could. So what are you going to do with yourself now that you're unemployed?" Julia asked, not so subtly changing the subject.

"I've got a nice nest egg and I can afford to open my own practice, even if it doesn't take off for a while. I'm going to look at leasing some office space—maybe within someone's office to cut costs. It's time I did something for me."

"Not your father?"

Mallory leaned her head back against the couch. "You mean you knew all along that the partnership track wasn't what I wanted?"

Julia's familiar blue eyes stared back at her. "You were using it as a way to make your father proud when nothing's going to get him to focus on anyone but himself. Meanwhile you convinced yourself you were happy. Who was I to argue?"

Mallory sighed. "You've got a point. But I'm over it now." And it had only taken her thirty years.

But she'd learned so much about herself that she could begin a brand-new life. Much as she wished Jack would be part of it, Mallory Sinclair was a fighter who thrived on a challenge. She'd survive.

But life would be so much brighter if Jack had learned the same lessons she had.

15

MALLORY HAD QUIT. Jack entered his private sanctuary slamming the door behind him so he could have a modicum of privacy in this gossip-stricken law office. Straight from the Hamptons, he'd been hit by a nasty summer flu and he'd missed another two days of work, bringing him into the weekend. He wished someone in this damn office had seen fit to tell him about Mallory while he was out sick.

He'd returned today, uncertain of how he'd deal with his office ice queen, knowing only that they weren't finished—to discover she was gone. The emptiness gnawing inside him was greater than any he'd experienced in the past.

But along with the void came an accompanying sense of pride in Mallory. She'd found herself on their business trip and as a result she finally saw herself as he did—as a woman who knows what she wants and isn't afraid to go after it.

The same way she'd gone after him. She wasn't afraid to walk away when her hopes, dreams, goals or desires weren't met. From a job or from him.

Jack glanced around his corner office, a status symbol by its very location. He took in the floor-to-ceiling windows and the gray, rainy New York City skyline, then turned to look at his mahogany desk, oversize leather chair, expensive oriental rug and handmade, wooden bookshelves—plus what felt like a lifetime's worth of mementos. His college and law school degrees, his New York State Bar admission and even his high school football jacket hung from the wall.

He'd started his law career right here. All his professional achievements were tied to this firm, but his time with Mallory had shown him he had no personal accomplishments to show for those same years. And suddenly his professional ones felt insignificant and lacking.

The mess with Lederman hadn't helped. He'd shown Paul the pictures, listened to his blustering and told him to think about the damage those photos could do to his business reputation. Jack expected to settle the case quickly and with a minimum of fuss—Lederman would get screwed and Jack wouldn't have to compromise his principles and push Paul's wife into an unfair settlement.

Jack stared out at the Empire State Building in the distance. He wouldn't be around here much longer either. From the moment he looked into Alicia Lederman's face and saw more than an adversary, more than someone he wanted to best in court, Jack knew his days with Waldorf, Haynes were numbered. Once again he had Mallory to thank for opening his eyes.

He couldn't blame the firm or even Lederman for his current dissatisfaction, he could only blame his unwillingness to face himself and his demons—and to accept the greatest gift offered to him.

Mallory's love.

"So what do you plan to do about it?" he asked himself.

He glanced at his too-neat desk and grabbed for a sheet of paper and pen. He'd get in touch with Mallory in words she couldn't misunderstand. Then he'd hope for the best.

HANDS ON HER HIPS, Mallory surveyed the office space available for rent from a friend of Julia's. He was an insurance agent with the extra room and a secretary with free time to lend her in exchange for the surplus income. It was cheaper than actually leasing space for herself. There was time enough for that huge step if she made a success of her new practice.

And she intended to. Mallory never did things halfway. Except for Jack. Somehow she'd blown that one.

Two weeks had passed since she'd left him behind and she hadn't heard a word. Not that she'd expected him to call but the dreamer—the one he'd brought out in her—had hoped. And there were times, mostly late at night, when she'd thought of calling him just to hear his voice, to see if he ached for her as much as she ached for him. But sanity would return and she'd remind herself that he knew she loved him. If during their time apart he realized he felt the same, he knew where to find her. There was nothing else she could say or do that would change things between them.

She walked out of the old building, pleased with the location but not ready to make the decision yet. A quick taxi ride home and she entered her apartment, tossing her bag down on the living room couch.

"Where have you been?" Julia came out of her room, impatience in her stride and in her voice.

"Checking out office space. But boy am I wiped out. This heat is a killer—not to mention that you can roast on the subway." Mallory flopped into the nearest chair.

"While you were gone I picked up the mail." Her cousin stood beside her and waited.

"And this is news because?"

"Of this!" Julia slapped an envelope onto Mallory's lap.

The ivory stationery had the familiar Waldorf, Haynes insignia and return address on the left hand corner, but that wasn't all. The attorneys scrawled their initials below the main address and her cousin hadn't missed the most important notation. The one that caused Mallory's heartbeat to accelerate and her pulse to pound hard.

"J.L. That's him, isn't it?" Julia asked, her voice rising in excitement.

"Mind if I read this in private?" Knowing she'd asked a rhetorical question and her cousin wasn't budging, Mallory ripped into the envelope as she spoke.

Julia stood over her shoulder and read aloud. "*One last time, a lifetime to share, I will be waiting—if you dare.* Oh my God, that's so romantic." Her accompanying shriek reverberated in Mallory's ear.

"So much for privacy," Mallory said wryly. A tremor shook her as she reread the words for herself and she agreed with her cousin. It was shocking and romantic and unbelievably scary.

Mallory didn't know what had prompted Jack's change of heart but she knew him well enough to realize he wouldn't have sent this letter unless he meant every word.

She turned the invitation over. The date was a week away, the address unfamiliar—and suburban.

"How does he expect you to get there?" Julia asked.

"Good question." Nothing on the paper indicated how Mallory would even find the place. She'd have to find a map for specific directions.

She fingered the paper between her fingers, imagining it held the warmth from Jack's touch. "But then I suppose nothing worth having is easy, right?"

Julia, unaware of the invitations that had passed between Mallory and Jack, merely nodded, looking a bit stunned.

Mallory wasn't shocked, she was certain. If she wanted him, she had to work to get him. *No one's ever gone out of their way for me.* She remembered the conversation clearly.

And though Mallory didn't think he was consciously making her work to get him, if she showed up as requested, he'd know without a doubt he was worth the effort.

It was a challenge—with a lifetime at stake.

MALLORY PARKED her rental car outside the address on the invitation. She checked the number on the mailbox twice to be certain, but the moment she'd seen the Victorian house with the white picket fence, she'd known she had the right place. Quaint and charming, the place spelled out *h-o-m-e*.

She stepped out of the car and into the rain, glancing around for a sign of something she recognized. Other than the tingling in her palms and the keen anticipation in her veins she always felt when Jack was near, nothing looked familiar.

Pulling up the hood and closing the lapels on her raincoat, she walked up to the front door. Though she'd never been a nail biter before, she was darn tempted to start now. Jack had issued the invitation but she'd added some special touches of her own. After their time apart, she was more nervous now than she'd been at the start. But she wanted him forever and he might as well know from the get-go the uptight Mallory was gone for good and nothing about *them* would ever be boring or predictable. She walked up the blue-stone steps and rang the bell.

JACK WATCHED HER pull up and opened the door at the same time the old bell sounded in the empty house. He thought he was dreaming as the object of his fantasies slipped past him and out of the rain.

She pushed back the hood and met his gaze, a hesitant smile on her lips. She held out the invitation for him to see. "I'm assuming I have the right place."

The right place and the right man. "I'm glad you found it okay."

She shrugged. "I never told you about my poor sense of direction but thanks to the Internet I made out okay. Can't get lost with door-to-door directions."

They stood in awkward silence. *Not* how he'd planned this meeting to go when he'd been without her too long. Jack stepped back to take her in. Her dark hair fell around her face in natural waves while her skin glowed from a combination of summer tan and perfectly applied cosmetics.

He had no idea what she wore beneath the trench coat but from what he could see she wasn't Mallory the associate nor was she Mallory the seductress.

She was *his* Mallory and if he didn't get her in his arms soon he'd howl with frustration. "I missed you."

Her hesitant smile turned into a grin. "Well it's about time you realized it," she said, and threw herself into his arms.

He buried his face in her hair and held on tight. Her scent was the same and so was the fulfillment he found just being near her.

She pulled back too soon. "So what is this place?" she asked, glancing around the empty house.

She had no idea what a huge question she'd posed. "Why don't you take your coat off and I'll explain."

The color heightened in her cheeks. "Not yet. I'm still cold."

He narrowed his gaze, then shrugged. "As long as you're not planning a quick escape."

"Trust me. I didn't drive all the way out here just to run off."

He grabbed for her hand, then met her gaze, grateful to be able to look into those blue eyes again. "I do trust you. With my life."

Her eyes filled with moisture as she reached a hand

out to his cheek. "That can't be an easy thing for you to say."

"Funny, but with you it is." He struggled for the right words.

She must have understood because she waited quietly.

"That week we spent together changed everything."

She inclined her head. "Tell me about it," she said softly.

He laughed. "I guess we both had a life altering experience. You found yourself and what you wanted out of life. I found you and learned that relationship isn't a dirty word." It wasn't just the sensual experiences they'd shared but the emotional bonding they'd done in the process, Jack thought. "By the time you left I realized I *couldn't* be the Terminator any more than I wanted to be."

Her intense stare never wavered. "Alicia said you were incredible."

He shook his head. "She was the incredible one. Just as you'd said. I just got damn lucky Lederman screwed himself because otherwise I'd have been in an untenable position. I couldn't walk away from that case without costing the firm and I'd never do that. Even though by then I had a hunch things were over for me there, too."

"You quit?" Her voice rose in pitch and shock.

"I'm in the process of selling my interest in the partnership. There's no way I can go on the way I've been, taking cases, helping to destroy marriages no matter the cost.'' He grinned. ''Not when I've seen the light.''

''I'm floored.''

''So am I. I'm still not certain which direction to take next but I am sure I did the right thing.''

''And this place?''

He couldn't stall any longer. His palms might be sweating like a teenager but he was a man on a mission and damned if he'd back down now. ''A gamble. You were on the fast track to partnership and insisted marriage and family didn't fit into the equation.'' He drew a deep breath. ''But you always believed and wanted me to believe, too. Now I do.''

''What are you saying?''

He clenched and unclenched his fists. ''I'm saying that when you gave up your job, I figured you were thinking about things differently. This is it, sweetheart. Your invitation to the American dream. The house, the white picket fence...''

He pointed toward the window facing outside. ''There's an animal shelter around the corner and I know I wouldn't mind getting started on the two-point-five kids. Of course I wouldn't keep you barefoot and pregnant. That mind's too sharp to waste, but I'm sure this town could use two more brilliant attorneys.''

She blinked in stupefied, stunned silence. There was a time he'd be grateful to have been able to shock her but no more. Control was not a damn illusion and she was in command.

And the longer her silence continued the more he wondered if he'd overestimated *them*. ''I don't own it yet so if you don't like it or want to stay in the city or don't want to get married…''

"What do you know, you ramble. I've never heard you nervous before.'' A wide grin spread slowly across her face.

Jack had his answer. He just wanted to hear the words. "So what do you say?''

"That my dreams have come true.'' In her wildest imagination, she'd never envisioned this kind of happily ever after, not for herself. And especially not for herself and Jack.

"And I love you.''

"I love you, too.'' He spoke without hesitation.

Mallory smiled. She was so lucky to have found a man who thought she was worth the effort of digging beneath the surface. And he deserved to be rewarded.

She began a slow unbuttoning of her coat, her trembling fingers hindering the attempt. "I just hope you're not expecting me to be the Mallory from the office, or a Stepford wife.'' Because she'd learned she was a combination platter and she was still discovering more about herself every day.

She shrugged the long coat off her shoulders and let it pool at her feet. He took in the sexy black lingerie she'd picked with him in mind and his eyes darkened with appreciation.

He let out a slow whistle. "Don't let the neighbors see you.''

She laughed. "I guess you'll have to install blackout shades,'' she said and crooked a finger his way.

"I take it that's a yes to my invitation?''

Her heart pounded hard in her chest. "That's yes to a lifetime."

Jack stepped forward, lifting her into his arms and sealing their bargain with a long, lingering kiss—a kiss that promised a lifetime of erotic invitations to come.

WITH HARLEQUIN AND SILHOUETTE

There's a romance to fit your every mood.

Passion
Harlequin Temptation

Harlequin Presents

Silhouette Desire

Pure Romance
Harlequin Romance

Silhouette Romance

Home & Family
Harlequin
American Romance

Silhouette
Special Edition

A Longer Story
With More
Harlequin
Superromance

Suspense &
Adventure
Harlequin Intrigue

Silhouette Intimate
Moments

Humor
Harlequin Duets

Historical
Harlequin Historicals

Special Releases
Other great
romances
to explore

CALL THE ONES YOU LOVE OVER THE HOLIDAYS!

Save $25 off future book purchases when you buy any four Harlequin® or Silhouette® books in October, November and December 2001,

PLUS

receive a phone card good for 15 minutes of long-distance calls to anyone you want in North America!

WHAT AN INCREDIBLE DEAL!

Just fill out this form and attach 4 proofs of purchase (cash register receipts) from October, November and December 2001 books, and Harlequin Books will send you a coupon booklet worth a total savings of $25 off future purchases of Harlequin® and Silhouette® books, AND a 15-minute phone card to call the ones you love, anywhere in North America.

Please send this form, along with your cash register receipts as proofs of purchase, to:
In the USA: Harlequin Books, P.O. Box 9057, Buffalo, NY 14269-9057
In Canada: Harlequin Books, P.O. Box 622, Fort Erie, Ontario L2A 5X3
Cash register receipts must be dated no later than December 31, 2001.
Limit of 1 coupon booklet and phone card per household.
Please allow 4-6 weeks for delivery.

I accept your offer! Enclosed are 4 proofs of purchase. Please send me my coupon booklet and a 15-minute phone card:

Name: _____

Address: _____ City: _____

State/Prov.: _____ Zip/Postal Code: _____

Account Number (if available): _____

---

097 KJB DAGL
PHQ4013